Passengers

Cassandra Swiderski

iUniverse, Inc.
Bloomington

Passengers

iUniverse books may be ordered through booksellers or by contacting:

iUniverse
1663 Liberty Drive
Bloomington, IN 47403
www.iuniverse.com
1-800-Authors (1-800-288-4677)

ISBN: 978-1-4502-8696-1 (sc)
ISBN: 978-1-4502-8697-8 (ebk)

Library of Congress Control Number: 2011900107

Printed in the United States of America

iUniverse rev. date: 01/18/2011

The higher you rise, the harder you fall.—Age-Old Saying

For of all sad words of tongue or pen,
The saddest are these: It might have been.—John Greenleaf Whittier

Actions only speak louder than insincere words.—C.S.

H:

I've never understood you
I've never ceased loving you,
If I could, I would
But we do what we're used to.
You're more than a stranger
or just a fellow passenger,
I'll wait for you in heaven
At the gate of endless passion.
Don't wonder about me
If you've left me in misery,
My heart has died
But deep down inside
Our love still breathes.

-A.

Dedication:

You know this is for You...

Because of you, reality is better than my imagination

--Cassandra

Passengers

Part One:

Holden & Anna

1

_A_fter all of these years, I've finally concluded my theory on life itself. We are all passengers on a train. Some of us enjoy the ride, looking out the window, gazing into the eyes of strangers, as though we prefer not to be in control. Then, there are the rest of us, myself included. My stomach twists and turns at the thought of all that I don't control in my own life. Why should I even refer to it as my own? It isn't, it belongs to someone else. Perhaps God, perhaps not. I care not to discuss semantics right now. For this isn't a story of theology, it is one of love. But, if God is the conductor of the train of life, please tell Him to pull the fucking thing over, I'm getting off.

You see, I am not bitter because I've never had love. I've experienced it to the fullest, like few people ever get to. My toils have resulted from the three greatest years of my life, the time I had with Holden Percy.

We met in December of 1927. No, this was not a May-December romance. Nor will it amaze you because of some seemingly fateful coincidence that brought us together. See, our love was _real_. But, I suppose my greatest friend Paul is right, had it been love, Holden and I would still be together. Paul is constantly telling me to appreciate the time we had. I can see Paul coming upon me now.

"Jesus, Anna, at least you had three years together, three years! It wasn't like it was just one night or something," he'd say.

"Or something's right, Paul," I always embellished every word I uttered with my trademark cynicism. Paul flooded his past with one-night stands. I would never pity him for it though, he should have known better. But then again, so should I. I wish someone had shook the living ghost out of me when I met Holden. Told me it wasn't real, told me it would end. But no one did. My bitterness is making me fat.

"Are you still with me in this conversation, Anna? Or am I wasting my time?" Paul was so impatient. "You had his love!"

"That's right, Paul. I *had* his love. Past tense! I don't have him now. Not his love, not the memories, not the fucking undying devotion! It's him I want."

I lit up a cigarette and inhaled slowly, ensuring every inch of smoke current would crawl down my throat.

"What are you doing?" Paul exclaimed, ripping the tobacco roll from my dry lips. "That crap will kill you."

"No it won't, Paul. I'm already dead."

I needed to get back to writing. Maybe if I laid some of these emotions on paper, I could calm down. I wasn't always like this you know, cynical, cruel, faultfinding. I used to be a good friend, a great friend, especially to Paul. We'd been through so much together. He had only one sibling, a sister, Nancy, but she died when he was seven. I won't be able to live with myself much longer if I continue to treat people as I have. I've disgusted myself to the point that I wish I never even met Holden. But if you only knew how carefree my heart used to be, you'd understand how I feel now.

I was fifteen when we met. I was twice promoted in school though, so I was in the middle of my senior year. On weekends, I worked at the public library in Topeka, Kansas. I actually live in Carson City, but it's only a twenty minute ride to Topeka. Nothing pleased me more than working at the library. If there were two things in the world I loved as much as God, they were helping people and studying literature. I had always wanted to be a writer. By my teenage years I had already authored two novels. My parents weren't interested much in my writing, they just looked at it as a 'fun little hobby.' The only person who understood how I felt was my sister, Mary. Like many girls, she dreamt of being a ballerina. But she did more than just dream. Every day she practiced until her routines were perfect. It was amazing, she even had the hair of a ballerina. It was always smoothed back into a little bun, spun beautifully, like a cinnamon roll. You could imagine my parents' reaction though. They expected nothing more of Mary and me than to get married and be spectacular wives. I didn't care about being any man's wife, let alone a spectacular one, until I met Holden.

It's so cliché to say that it was love at first sight, but it'd be a lie to say otherwise. A girl I worked with at the library, Carmen, was always urging me to let one of my teachers see my books. I knew they'd have the same reaction as my parents though. Then, one December afternoon she trampled into the library, hurriedly taking off her wool coat and rabbit's fur mittens.

"Carmen, get those wet boots away from the new books," shouted our supervisor, Elliot.

"Anna, wait till you hear this."

"I'm listening."

"Alex's brother is an author himself. He even won the Golden Pen Award when he went to U of K, but he doesn't go there anymore. Anyway, that doesn't matter. What *does* matter is that I was telling him all about you and he wants to meet you. Isn't that great? He has so many great ideas for stories, and he's really smart and all, so I'm sure--"

"Why doesn't he go to school if he wants to be an author?" It really bothered me that men had so many opportunities, but didn't take advantage of them. If I could, I was going to get a college degree.

"I don't know, Anna. I guess he doesn't have time. So do you want to meet him or what?"

"I guess." I was interested in anything that could benefit me as a writer. Even if it cost me a little dignity or time.

"Terrific. Alex and Aaron are having a dinner party Friday night. You can come. Wear green or red, it's a Christmas theme!"

I had to get away from the giddiness of Carmen. I used to love being around her, but ever since she met Alex, I think he's sucked her brain out through her lips. We used to talk about so many different things, poetry, dreams, women's history. Now, everything revolves around Alex. My mother says I'm jealous, but actually, I'm disappointed. Carmen could have amounted to being so much more than a wife.

Plus, I wasn't too thrilled about this dinner party. People talking as if they're brilliant. They'll discuss books, when we all know quite well that they're just regurgitating a synopsis that a friend heard from another friend who spewed out the same story. Alex and Aaron were also about the two snootiest people I had ever met. They both graduated from Harvard, and returned to Kansas to save us all by setting up some law establishment. They knew if they stayed out East they'd both be a couple of nobodies. But in Carson City, they were the hometown heroes.

Paul encouraged me to be optimistic about meeting Alex's brother. It slipped my mind to even ask Carmen his name, which really bothered me. I wouldn't want to be known as Jeffrey's daughter, anymore than I'm sure he wants to be recognized as Alex's little shadow. I prayed they were polar opposites.

My grandmother once warned me to watch what I wished for, and be dead serious about what I prayed for. She was right. The moment I met Holden, everything in me changed. I began to breathe different, walk different, and for some reason, my smile broadened. I was naive, but not as much as most girls my age. I knew that this was love. He seemed so calm and collected when he reached for my hand, as though he had prepared for this moment his entire life.

"Anna Marters, I'm Holden," his voice was very smooth and masculine. I bet he even had perfect pitch.

"It's a pleasure to meet you. Carmen tells me you're an author yourself."

"Well, I hope to be an author someday."

"Don't say that. You don't have to be making a living at something to be considered what you already are."

He smiled at me and I could tell that no one had ever made him feel at peace the way that I had just done.

"Maybe we could exchange novels and share ideas and opinions."

"Of course, I'd love to hear what you've learned about writing thus far."

"I meant our opinions on anything and everything. You know, whatever you'd like to discuss...Carmen's told me so much about you, Anna. I'm certain we could talk for hours."

"Sure, in fact--"

"Anna, come meet Alex's friends."

"Right now? Carmen, I'm busy!" I was no longer appearing nonchalant. Carmen was ignoring the plea that crept through my grinding teeth.

I only talked to Holden one more time before leaving the party. We didn't even sit together for dinner, but I could see him glancing at me out of the corner of my eye. On my way out the door he asked to meet me at the local diner in Carson City, a week from Saturday. I believe he said 6 o'clock, but I was so distracted by his indigo eyes that I wasn't certain. That didn't bother me though. I figured it would be better anyway if I were an hour or two early. I'd have enough time to rehearse what I would tell him about my novels and my goals for the future. Yet, when he arrived that evening, I'd forgotten everything I planned to say.

"Anna, so good to see you again."

"You too." I motioned with my eyes to the chair across from me, hoping he would sit down. I never liked speaking to men while they were standing up and I was sitting down. It made me feel inferior. But after talking to Holden that night, I knew that I would never feel that way again around him. He was always interested in what books I read, plays I've seen, songs I've written. He complimented me on my ambition and intelligence, never once mentioning my looks.

I couldn't wait until I saw him again. I was already deeply in love. I'm telling you, nothing bothered me from that point on. In fact, it amazed me how many people were disturbed by the weather, traffic jams, or long lines at the cinema. Being stranded allowed me more time to think of him. I went home and wrote my first song about Holden. How I wanted to sing it for him, telling him with my voice and tiny fingers how I felt. I would hum into ecstasy and pluck my guitar with the gentleness only of a woman in love.

But I couldn't. It was too soon. I couldn't believe myself. I had never acted this way before. Now I see why Carmen has a smile etched onto her face. Holden gave me this feeling of fulfilled passion by just talking to me. One glance at him and I realized why I was living.

"Anna," he asked me the following weekend. "Do you believe in God?"

"Of course I do."

"No, really. Tell me what He means to you."

My mind went blank. I felt so on the spot. How could I explain such a vast influence in my life in a few mere sentences? So, instead, I said nothing at all. Holden seemed odd the rest of that afternoon. I feared that he'd changed how he felt for me. He never told me I was special to him, but I was sure that I was. All that week I couldn't sleep or eat. My mother kept hassling me to finish my chores, but I just sat on the linoleum kitchen floor and cried silently. I prayed no one would hear me, and run in and ask, "what's wrong?" a thousand times over. Thank God, no one did.

I sat by the phone waiting for Holden to call, expecting him to say we couldn't see each other anymore. He never called. Instead, he showed up at my door Saturday morning, and asked me to take a ride with him. He didn't seem mad at all. I couldn't believe this. Had he forgotten my answer to his question? I pretended as though nothing was wrong. After we drove for an hour, discussing our week's affairs, he pulled off onto a dirt road and got out of his car.

"Anna, come with me." He held out his hand and I clutched onto it. We walked through a grass field for about five minutes when I noticed something up ahead. "I thought it'd be nice if we had a little picnic together and talked some more about what I asked you last week."

"Okay," I uttered with a half-smile. *I'm a goner now,* I thought. I anxiously tried to think of a mature sounding response, but nothing quite came to mind. Then, I remembered what I heard Mr. Ainsley say at church one afternoon, how God had intervened in his life in so many ways, and that Mr. Ainsley owed all goodness to God for being there for him, even when he was doubtful. I figured this was as good of an answer as any, so I prepared my speech.

"What's wrong, Anna? You look like you're constructing a bridge in your head."

"Oh, I'm fine," I giggled. I was never good at hiding my emotions. When I was nervous, everyone around me knew.

"Look, I'm not expecting you to have all the answers, or even *an* answer. I just want you to speak to me from your heart. Tell me who you are and what you feel. God made you smart and beautiful, and so very kind. You're one of the sweetest people I've ever known."

I felt my face percolating. I had to interrupt and rationalize.

"Well, you've probably known a lot of great girls, so that's very kind of you to say. Thank you, Holden...you know, for the compliment?"

He had a strange look in his eyes, quite mischievous.

"What? *Hol*den!"

"How many girls do you think I've, um, *known*, Anna?"

"Oh, sorry, I didn't mean it like that."

"Don't apologize."

"I know, I know, I'm so apologetic, people tell me that all the time."

"It's not that I mind, I don't dislike anything about you."

"You don't?"

"No. Why, should I?"

"No, not at all."

"You can tell me anything, you know. I won't judge you."

"Please, everyone says that. What if I told you I was a horrible person, that I'd intentionally lied and hurt someone's feelings before? Then you'd want to know why I did it."

"No, I wouldn't. I'd just ask you if you sought God for His forgiveness."

"Do you believe God forgives anything?"

"If you confess your sins and you're truly sorry, and He knows when you are, then you will be forgiven."

"I have."

"I know."

2

*H*olden dropped me off at home and assured me that he'd call during the week. I felt so peaceful and content. No, what I really felt was acceptance. Regardless of what I said to Holden he still cared about me. No one had ever offered me such unconditional approval, not even my parents.

I spent that week daydreaming about my picnic with Holden, the way he'd stare into my eyes when I talked, and smiled anytime I blushed. I thought about telling him that I loved him, but it was too soon. I didn't want him to think I was so casual about uttering such a loaded phrase.

"Anna, you've really been slacking off this week," joked Elliot. "What's been on your mind?"

"Oh, just this book concept I have."

"Sure, sure, a book idea, right."

By the smirk on his face I could tell that Elliot knew. I figured that I might as well tell him the details. You never know when you'll need advice later on from such a smart guy. Elliot always encouraged me to follow my heart, no matter what the odds were: go to college, be a writer, I could do anything. I sensed he'd tell me to do the same with Holden, heart over head.

"I am so in love, Elliot, I mean smitten! I have never felt this way before, this is it, he's the one, I'm certain, I--"

"Hold on, catch your breath kiddo. Who is 'he'?"

"You know Carmen's boyfriend Alex? His brother, Holden. He's--"

"Whoa, look, Anna, I like Carmen a lot, but she's, well, different from you. I'm not sure you should be going out with a guy like Alex."

"No, he's nothing like his brother. He's warm and thoughtful and articulate and he's fond of *me*!"

"I'm not surprised."

"I am."

"What's wrong with you? You're a terrific girl. Everyone I know would love to have you date their son. You're smart, ambitious, pretty, polite, and you *used* to be a hard worker."

"Elliot!"

"It's okay. We're all allowed to act like fools somewhat when we're in love. Just don't let it ruin what you've got going for you."

"I won't! Why does everyone say that?"

"Because we care about you and we know what kind of potential you have. Anna, you're like no other teenager I've ever known. You could do anything. I just don't want to see you stop caring about your dream because of this guy, that's all."

"This guy? This guy *is* my dream. He's everything I've ever wanted. I know how young I am, but believe me I know. I felt it the moment we met. He won't hold me back at all because he thinks I'm gifted. I won't change, except for the better."

"Promise?"

"Promise."

"Okay, kiddo. Back to work."

After work I stopped at the bookshop before going home. I wanted to buy a copy of T.S. Eliot's *The Love Song of J. Alfred Prufrock*. Holden told me all about it, how it was a sort of pathetic modern love song which few people had read. Holden said it inspired him to write some poetry, and I knew it would do the same for me. It was stunning how alike we were.

"Anna, is that you? Your dinner's in the warmer."

"Thanks, Mama."

I had to sneak in the book, if Mama knew that I bought a book instead of checking one out for free from the library, she would have been furious. Money's like a grenade, she and Daddy always said, once you let go of it, you can't ever get it back whole again. But I never believed that books were a waste of money. I needed the research to help me be a better writer. They never understood that. I heard Mary dancing down the stairs. I let out a chuckle when I saw her, all dressed up with no place to dance off to. She crept over to me on her tiptoes.

"He called for you," she whispered in my ear.

I wanted to scream, but I could hear my father coming through the screen door.

"Oh my gosh!" I shoveled in my dinner as fast as I could.

"Be careful there, Anna Ellen, you'll choke to death," my father's words pulled me out of my daydream. I could tell more words were ready to leap from his lips. "Besides, you're not even enjoyin' it. That's good food there an' you're just heavin' it in like a pig."

Mary laughed at my amusing Daddy. I didn't care, I just wanted to call Holden before it was too late. I ran to the back guest room and dragged the phone into the bathroom, locking the door behind me. I could hear my father ask Mary what was wrong with me. I didn't even fancy a guess at her answer. None of this mattered. I only wanted to hear Holden's voice.

"Hello?"

I could tell right away that it was he.

"Let us go then, you and I, when the evening is spread out against the sky."

"You found *Prufrock*!"

"Yes."

"Don't you love it?"

"I don't know. I mean, so far I do. But I haven't had a chance to read much yet." I felt myself growing brave. This boy had no idea what he'd done for my self-confidence level. "I'll tell you what I do love though."

"What?"

"You. I love *you* Holden!...Holden?...Are you there?"

"Yeah, I'm here."

"Did I say something wrong? I--"

"I love you too, Anna."

I swallowed my heart. It didn't matter what we'd say now, there was nothing that could outdo those words. I twirled my soft hair, closed my eyes, and curled up into a little ball on the cold floor. The tiles were broken and poked my feet but it did not matter. Holden loved me and I was sure now. I remember that moment vividly, he began talking about some Michelangelo photo he saw at the bookshop, and how his parents were pressing him to return to school. I sort of half-listened to the rest of the conversation. All I could do was stare at my ivory face and widened eyes in the medicine cabinet mirror. I smiled while Holden continued talking, my eyelashes spreading out like tiny fingers reaching upward. God had something better planned for me than the life I was currently living. He sent Holden specially to be with me, and for the first time in my life, I wanted to be a man's wife.

3

The following morning I burst out of bed. I grabbed my little notebook that I always carried with me, ran downstairs, and kissed my mother goodbye. That evening I had to work a shift at the library to do inventory. It didn't even bother me that my day lasted nearly seventeen hours. When I got home I didn't expect to see anyone up. My parents both go to sleep fairly early, and Mary was probably getting her beauty rest as well. I stumbled onto the porch steps, my eyes only half open. Then I realized there was somebody behind me.

"Anna, goodnight."

"Holden. What are you doing here?"

"I came to say goodnight to you."

"Oh. Goodnight, sweetheart."

"What's that?"

"What?"

"In your hand?"

"Oh, just a poem I was working on at work."

"Can I see it?"

"Not yet. Not until it's finished, okay?"

"Alright. Well, goodnight."

"You came an awful long way just to tell me that."

"Nah, it was worth it."

Holden reached for my hand. He often kissed it lightly, the way a gentleman does in the movies. I slipped a tiny piece of paper into his hand after his lips parted my skin.

"What's this, love?"

"Bedtime reading."

I smiled at him and reminded myself to capture the moment in my mind's treasure chest.

I crept upstairs careful not to wake anyone. For a moment, I paused and wondered what my family dreamt of. I knew exactly what I would be imagining. Tumbling into bed with my clothes still on, I recalled the note I placed into Holden's hand. It read: We Are One.

4

*R*egret should be a four letter word. That's why I refer to it as "gret." So often, it makes people take paths that they would never ordinarily choose in their lives.

"I should have finished college," Holden muttered to me over scrambled eggs one Saturday. We met at the same family diner as we had before. It felt completely natural to talk to Holden about his fears and apprehensions. I knew that our relationship was growing serious quickly, but I wasn't worried.

"You shouldn't blame yourself for what you have or haven't done, Holden. There are things we all wish we could do over again, but we can't. You've made the best of your time so far, and I'm positive that God is pleased by that."

Holden looked stunned. I tried to mentally recite the words that just flew out of my mouth to see if I said anything inappropriate. He could tell my wheels were turning.

"Uh, what's wrong?"

"Oh, nothing. You seemed upset or shocked or something about what I said so I was trying to recall if I said something that would have disappointed you."

This time he looked even more stunned. What kind of hole was I digging myself into?

"Anna," he paused, "you said nothing wrong. It was comforting, just what I *needed* you to say. You really shouldn't worry so much about what I think. Just be yourself, alright? I promise if you do that, nothing will go wrong."

His smile always soothed my anxious personality. Like every other woman I knew, I had this 'aiming to please everyone' quality. But Holden really accepted me the way I was. I felt there was nothing I could do to lose him.

"Holden? Do you think you'll ever get married?"

He looked up from his eggs. His toast crust drooped into his coffee cup. *Wonderful, Anna*, I thought. *You're on a roll today.*

"We're going to get married. You know that don't you?"

I had been outdone. My mouth was wide open but I was gasping for air. For the first time in my life I didn't fear my future.

"I have something serious I need to talk to you about."

"Huh?" Holden awoke me from my momentary hallucination. I was counting my bridesmaids.

"Listen, Anna, I might be leaving for a while."

"How long!"

"Don't worry, probably just a few months. I'm taking a trip to Omaha to meet a publisher. He's going to review two of my novels and fund for me to go to an intensive writing workshop. I have to do it. I *want* to do it, I think he's really going to help me. These are very difficult times, love, and this man's willing to fund for *me* to be a better craftsman. This is really a once in a lifetime opportunity. But don't worry, I'll never forget you and I'll write you a little every day...It'll be alright."

Holden wiped the tears from my cheek that I hadn't even realized fell. Up until this moment I had felt confident in our relationship. All of a sudden, I was terrified. I had hoped that Holden couldn't tell, but I knew the transparency of my fragile body. I pretended to be happy for him, but inside, I feared for the worst.

5

"How do you say goodbye to someone you love so much?"

"Anna, he'll come back for you, I know it. Alex said that Holden was extremely upset about going because he doesn't want to leave you."

"Carmen, I *know* we're meant to be together. What if he meets someone when he's in Omaha, some mature, enchanting writer who's beautiful and rich and--"

"Don't worry, he won't."

It was Holden's voice. I knew that eventually I had to turn around and confront him, but I was taking my time. My face was so hot that I could feel the lipstick peeling off my lips.

"Holden! What a surprise. So good to see you." I reached out my hand and smiled excitedly.

"What am I, your boyfriend or your agent? Come give me a hug, Anna."

I fell into his arms. He was always so warm and comfortable. My fingers scrolled through his rich blond hair, and I trembled as his dry, ink-stained hands gently caressed my shoulder blades. It was the most passionate, erotic moment of my life, and we hadn't even kissed yet.

"Holden, I love you," I breathed into his ear.

"I know, Anna." He cupped my chin with his left thumb and forefinger. "It's only a matter of time."

Someone once said that eyes are the windows to a person's soul. Whoever that was, was dead on. I looked at those innocent indigos for what seemed to be at least five minutes, and I was certain. Holden would come back for me.

"I have something to give you. Can we go for a short walk?"

I looked around for Elliot and spotted him immediately. By now, the entire library staff was standing around, dissecting our spectacle. Elliot waved over to us, motioning that I could leave work to carry on with my "dreamboy," as he referred to Holden.

The moment we stepped outside, I glimpsed Holden falling.

"Are you alright?" I extended my hand to help him up.

"I haven't fallen, well, except for you." *Uncomfortable laughter.* He reached into his pocket and I knew exactly what was going to happen. I almost wished that he had done this inside, Carmen would have shrieked.

"I want you to have this." A gold chain fell into my palm. It was cold and quite heavy, and not *exactly* what I had expected. Surprisingly though, I wasn't disappointed once I realized what it was.

"My mother gave me that cross the evening after my grandmother's funeral. She would have wanted me to have it, that's what my parents said anyway. I was only seven, but I remember how much better I felt to have something of hers around my neck, covering my heart. It's your now. I want you to wear it while I'm gone and anytime you feel lonely just press it to your chest and know that I will warm you through this cross. Anna, no one has ever connected to me the way that you have. And I want you to rest assured that I'm coming back for you. No matter what trials we have nor what distance may separate us, I will always come back...I will always come back."

I couldn't speak. *Thank you, God,* I thought.

6

could always count on my parents to disapprove.

"What's that around your neck, Anna?" my mother inquired at dinner that evening.

"Don't *even* tell me you bought that. You're supposed to be saving your money for college."

"Daddy, I am. It's from a man I met."

I had to pause, Mary began giggling. I knew it was torturing her keeping this secret. My parents always somehow knew the happenings of my life even if I didn't announce them, so I figured that they noticed my behavior changes. I couldn't stop smiling.

"What man?" My father stabbed his mashed potatoes with his fork, like a killer to his corpse. He pushed the food around on his plate, forcing it onto the table, like the blood spewing from the dead body.

"His name's Holden and *he's a genius*! He's a writer *and* we met through friends *and* he's going to a special program for novelists *and* he's so generous, I just *know* that you're going to love him!"

"Don't count your chickens before they hatch."

My father chewed a piece of chicken loudly, as if it were my mother's rubbery Sunday roast. He didn't even need to say anything more, I knew they wouldn't like Holden. None of my friends have a chance with my parents, which is why I no longer have many friends.

My father is so suspicious of people that it crossed my mind to ask him if he was a Communist.

"Father, are you a--"

"A what?"

"Um, all done? I was going to wash up the dishes and hit the sack. I'm beat!"

"Does it look like I'm done? Just because you're makin' me lose my appetite doesn't mean I'm gonna throw away this food which cost me a hour's work to earn."

"Sorry. May I be excused?" I noticed that Mary didn't even ask. She just crept out of the room as my father was murdering his chicken...again.

"Yes, you may, dear." Thank God my mother wanted to change the subject.

"We're not done discussing this boy."

"He's a man!"

"Oh, even better! You listen to me young lady, and don't interrupt." I was too terrified to interrupt, I hate it when he shouts in his raspy farmer voice. My back tingles and my hands shake, I try not to look him in the eye, but the force is already over me. "You'll see *who* I tell you to see, *when* I tell you to see them. Understand?" I swear the windows shook he was screaming so loud.

"No! I love him, you don't--"

"Love! You think you know what love is? Come here!" My eyes were blurry from the waterfall of tears. I was so scared I was tempted to run, but I knew better. Again I fell, but this time I wasn't sure what hit me. Cold, syrupy blood crawled down my cheek.

"Jeffrey, look at her face."

My parents began arguing amongst themselves. I was so lightheaded that I thought I was going to lose consciousness. With my face pressed in the hall carpet, I army crawled to the bathroom. I didn't clean off my face, I just laid on the tiles, my only hearth.

Why was this happening? How could love be so comforting and rewarding, but also indigestible? Wasn't love always good, always a blessing?

Time passed, but I hadn't a clue how much. I had to get up, the blood was drying to my face and the floor was too warm now to sooth me. I wiped my flesh off hoping no marks were visible. The last thing I needed now was everyone at work asking, 'what's wrong' a thousand times over.

"Honey, are you alright?" My mother's voice in all its maternal bliss, her fist pounding the cheap wooden bathroom door, aching to touch my wound.

"I'm okay, Mama." I opened the door. "I need to rest, I'm going to bed."

"Sleep well, angel."

"You too, Mama...Mom, doesn't Daddy know I won't love him any less? Holden means a lot to me, but he's not replacing anyone."

"I know. He'll come around. All you and Holden can do to prove yourselves is stand the test of time."

7

My dearest Holden,

I miss you so much darling, my heart aches! I absolutely cannot wait until I can kiss your lips again and hold your strong hands within my own. Last night I dreamt of meeting you at the station, anxiously gripping my white gloves, taking frequent short breaths awaiting your arrival. How disappointed I was to wake up and realize that would not be my fate for the day.

Everything's well here. Mary's teaching two dance classes for local youth this summer. Mama's fine, nothing new with her. Daddy's repossessed my necklace from you, but don't worry, he'll come around. I was tempted to steal it off his nightstand, but I didn't.

Anyway, you <u>must</u> write and tell me all you're learning, and send any samples of your new works.

I love you, Holden.

Yours still,
Anna

My sweet Anna,

So good to get your letter, an angel left it on my pillow? I really am learning an exorbitant amount on literature and grammar. You would

love it here. I've begun to write a science fiction piece based in 2030.
Dr. Blizna says it may win a high prize at the end of the workshop.
Praise the Lord for that!"

I'm pleased to hear of Mary's success and that your parents are well.
While I am glad that you cherish the necklace, do not steal it back. You
have my love, even if you have no material item bearing it. No one could
take that away from you.

Love,
Your Holden

The entire duration of Holden's trip was viewed by my parents as an opportunity to convince me of my mistake. They refer to the love I have with Holden as momentarily satisfying, naive, and hormonal. I constantly rebuked every label they branded upon us, but I began to be concerned that when Holden returned he'd be driven away by the cruel persistence of my parents, which *I* had grown accustomed to.

The days passed by rather quickly. Carmen expected me to be more depressed than I was, but loving Holden always made me happy. While I longed for him, absence makes the heart grow fonder, it is so true! The night before Holden's return, however, I was feeling particularly unsettled. I tried to relax and read, but I couldn't. My eyes skimmed past the words on the page, searching for his face. A bath didn't calm me either, nor did a cup of my mother's famous fruit tea. She stood at the kitchen counter dicing orange and lemon peels, always looking cautious even though she knew that I knew how restless her heart could be.

"Mother, I'm sorry, but I don't think the tea'll do much good. Why don't you enjoy it?"

"Alright."

"I don't know what to do with myself. I'm bursting with

excitement that Holden'll be back tomorrow night, but I feel like I have to keep my feelings stuffed inside of me like an innocent holiday turkey, otherwise Daddy'll...*devour* me!"

"Why don't you head out then for some fresh air?"

"Now?"

"Sure, why not?"

"It's nearly ten o'clock. If Daddy finds out..."

"*I* said you could go. Besides, he won't find out."

My mother held my chin with her hand the way Holden always had. I kissed her goodnight, then fled upstairs and threw on my dress pants and boots. I didn't even change my nightshirt. I just wanted to leave before my father heard me up still.

Of course I had no fathom of an idea where I was going, but I sprinted from my house as fast as I ever had. After walking for nearly two hours I was exhausted and weak, and decided to return home. My tongue was velcroed to the roof of my mouth I was so thirsty. I recalled a coffee and soda bar up the street a ways.

I walked in hoping that they'd grant me a glass of water. I expected it to be closed, perhaps a few cleaners and regulars left. Only my eyes caught me in a scene which I've never experienced prior to that moment. Dozens of strangers filled the smoky room. I know nearly two-thirds of the residents of Carson and none of these men looked vaguely familiar.

"God, just let me sneak out of here unnoticed." I turned and slowly pushed the creaky door open, but the crowd was quieter than when I had entered.

"Miss, can we help you?"

A mammoth, bearded redhead pointed directly at me, although I was the sole female present.

"No, I'm..." I couldn't speak. My throat was slowly closing in from the lack of saliva. I could just envision the blank look on my face when I recognized someone I knew.

"Paul? What are you doing here?"

He lifted his head, which hung heavily from drunkenness, and pushed his eyeballs through their swollen lids.

"Hey kid, how are ya?"

"Paul! *What* are you doing?"

"What does it look like I'm doing? I'm having a few drinks to forget about my life, *that's* what I'm doing. What are you doing--isn't it past your bedtime?"

Even though I was full aware of Paul's state, it really hurt that he insulted me. I'm used to the comments about my protective parents from other people, but Paul and I were friends. Or at least I thought we were.

"Oh I gotta stop this," he grumbled while wiping his face with his dirty hands.

"You should stop drinking, you have no reason to--" Even without trying I came off as a know-it-all. I hated that about myself.

"Hey, I have problems too, you know."

"Yeah?"

"Yeah. Her name is Lanna."

I was stunned, but recovered quickly. She was probably one of his overnight mistresses who stiffed him with the hotel bill.

"Who's Lanna?" I pretentiously inquired.

"Lanna? She's so many things. Too many to put into words. How can we expect words to capture what's cursing our heart? They're so weak."

"No, Paul. Words aren't weak, they're everything."

"You can't touch words the way you can a lover."

"Yes, you can! Paul...Paul, listen to me. You can touch words, unlike emotions. Feelings can never be seen nor caressed nor heard. Only expressed. And how do you express them, I ask...*through words*!"

Paul didn't care. He was too toasted now to have an intelligent conversation, or even an argument. It amazes me to discover violent words coming from a drunkard. They always seem lifeless and apathetic to me.

"Excuse me," I asked a man whom I presumed to be the owner (he was the only sober company I had in the establishment), "could we have a couple of coffees?"

"Sure, I just put a pot on."

"Thanks. Now Paul, tell me about Lanna."

"Lanna is the sick joke fate played on me. I met her three years ago and fell in love with her instantly. She has this thick gorgeous blond hair, and wide chestnut eyes. I knew I wanted to say something to her, but for once in my life I was terrified introducing myself. God couldn't have created a more perfect woman if He tried. She was stunning in every stride, each move she made grabbed hold of me like I was her puppet. I finally said hello to her, but that was all I said...Well, to make a long story short, she had more to say to me. How could such a woman be interested in a louse like myself, I do not know. But she was. Something about her crept under my skin and from that moment on, I believed that life wasn't just a series of meaningless chances...Destiny, God, fate, whatever you want to call it, drew us together. It was like we were bonded and even she and I couldn't break from this web of passion. I know this sounds like a bunch of BS, but it's not. I love her. I keep telling myself now that we're apart that I'll find someone else, but I know that I won't. She was the one. It just kills me, like someone gave me everything I ever wanted, but it was never really mine--"

"Like a dream?"

"No, because it was real, too real to be compared to a dream. More like dangling the panacea for heartache right in front of your face, then snatching it away after you've jumped through flaming hoops to reach it."

"I know what you're saying."

"Do you? I doubt it. I mean, I love ya kid, you're a terrific girl and a great friend and all, but you've never felt such heartache. Honestly, I hope you never do. I wouldn't wish this hell on my worst enemy. And trust me, I've got lots of those."

Paul forced himself to smile and I immediately realized that this was the truest of bonding experiences I had ever had with a friend. Reciting a tale of true love is a fate too few endeavor, though so many have endured.

8

$\mathcal{I}$ returned home wide awake at three a.m. Paul and I had shared buried emotions that I never expected us to have in common. After watching him pour out his pain from the depth of his bruised heart I began thinking about my relationship with Holden. As soon as I entered my room I wrote myself a brief list of what I wanted to tell him. I desperately did not want to become like Paul, sitting amongst alcohol-soaked strangers, expecting nothing more from life than the sun to rise and set. Maybe listening to Paul's story just shook my confidence a little. Holden said that nothing could ever change how he felt, and I believed him. But what choice did I have? *When in love, we must refuse the right to question suspicious promises.* I decided that I would lay myself on the line for Holden. I knew it could scare him away, but I didn't care. Sometimes acting on the moment allows us to shed our fronts in a way that we never could prepare for. If my heart was going to speak for me, I couldn't rehearse. This time I needed to ride the rails not knowing when to get off. When I'd feel the urge to stop, I'd jump to the tracks, hoping to land on my feet. If I didn't, I wouldn't blame myself. At least I tried to find a guarantee, well, as close of one as you can get in love.

"Holden!"

"Hey, Anna!"

I sprinted into his poised arms, ready for him to catch my fall. The wind broke abruptly, tearing the hat off of his sandy hair.

"I don't think I fully realized how much I missed you until this moment."

"Oh, Anna, I don't ever want to leave you again. I love you so much."

"I love you, too."

I struggled not to choke on the stream of salty tears swimming down my throat. Never had I expected that moment to nearly collapse over inexpressible emotions.

"Hungry?"

"What?" Like I could think of nourishment at such a time.

"Let's go to the diner and talk for a while, okay?"

"Sure."

For the first time, I didn't feel any need to be someone other than myself. I didn't concentrate on my monologue, nor did I sweat bullets when self-doubt crept upon me, terrifying my heart to scream out whom she loved.

When we arrived at the diner, I expected Holden to tell me all about his trip. For some reason though, he had nothing to say, nor did I. We sat facing each other, Holden gently caressing my defined knuckles.

"There's nothing to announce, because you know it already. My lips cannot express my heart's desires any better than they already have. I love you, Anna, you know that, right?"

"Yes, I do."

"What more do you need to know then?"

"What will become of us? When will we be together...all the time, I mean. I swear I will love you forever, if you will do the same."

"You said you knew that I loved you."

"Oh, I do, but will you love me *forever*?"

"Is there another kind of love?"

"It seems that there must be. So many people--"

"We aren't other people."

"Who are we then?"

"Two droplets of God's love, gently fallen from heaven, destined to love each other as we're meant to love Him."

I had an idea what Holden was saying, but I wasn't quite sure. He was such an optimist, even if he denied it.

"That's beautiful Holden, but if we're such destined lovers, why are we hurting so much to be apart?"

"That hurt is part of the love, they're one and the same--"

Right. I had heard this one before. It's not that I was intentionally being skeptical, but it always seemed absurd to me for someone to say two people who loved each other could not be together. For as timid as I knew I could be, at least I didn't live an existence cluttered with excuses.

"Holden, I want you, and if having you in my life means that I have to accept this pain as well--"

"Exactly--"

"That's fine, but how long must I hurt for? Should we both suffer apart, when being together would ease this pain? If I have it within me to sooth my heart, then I must do that. When I'm with you, I'm more than happy, God I hate that word, it expresses nothing...I'm ecstatic, and abounding in pure joy, and sheer of callous fronts, and more than anything, free! I'm free to laugh, and--"

"My dear Anna, sorrow is better than laughter."

"It is?" This was all news to me.

"Yes. For by the sadness of the countenance the heart is made better."

"Excuse me?" I never thought of myself as extraordinarily intelligent, but critical analysis was my specialty. "Could you say that again?"

He wrote something down, which I assumed was this loaded

phrase for me to study. He slid the paper across the table, I glanced at it 'Ecclesiastes 7:3.' Not surprising, Holden was quoting a Biblical lesson. Yet, I had never heard such a verse that described how I felt at a particular moment.

"Don't look so surprised, Anna. I told you there was something soothing about God's Word, didn't I?"

My moment of comfort was lost. Holden was at a level I was not. I didn't know if it was better to admit this or keep quiet, but my mouth never allowed me to hide an honest observation.

"Yes, you did say that...I just feel like you understand something, I'm not even quite sure *what*, but you have privy to something I don't."

"Well, that's why I love you. See, meant to be."

I read that passage over and over that night in bed. Something just clicked for me, and I was anxious to relay the good news to Holden. I pulled out the piece of paper he had given me with the scripture verse written on it, and turned it over to write him a message. Gasping, I realized I had seen this slip before. It read, 'We Are One,' the message I wrote that had bonded our hands weeks before. Holden had carried it with him all this time.

9

The following afternoon I left work early to drive to Holden's. I had to tell him about my revelation the previous night. I had never stopped by his home unannounced, but I didn't expect it to be a problem. The closer I arrived to the house, however, the more leery I began to feel. Thinking it would allow me the last minute option to leave before anyone saw me, I parked at the entrance of the gravel driveway. Their property was so large that I felt certain that nobody could see me. Holden's car was parked on the grass next to the oak tree, so I began to plunge through the dirt and stones to the front door. The door was open, so I thought about screaming through the screen, but I wasn't sure who else was home. Before knocking, my hand flinched. Someone inside was yelling, not Holden, but I was unfamiliar with the voice. I paused to collect myself from the shock, it was my luck that I stopped by during a heated family brawl. Holden never mentioned to me any family problems, thus I was taken aback by the language meandering inside.

There was a moment's pause, so I abruptly pounded on the metal rim of the screen door. At least I could rescue Holden from the opponents debating profanely.

A scruffy-haired, but well-dressed, man appeared in front of me out of nowhere, asking who I was and what I wanted. I tried to swallow the lump of air stuck in my throat, so it took me a moment to respond.

"Hi, um, is Holden around?"

"Yes, he's here."

"Could I see him for a moment, uh, I just wanted to tell him something."

"You must be his girl then."

"Yes, I am," I cheerfully responded, extending my hand as though his would come through the screen to welcome me. But he didn't move at all, not a word was uttered, we just stood there staring at each other. Mine was a friendly I-hope-you-like-me-if-you're-his-father look, his a suspenseful glare. He was trying to intimidate me, which was working quite well.

"Come on in, we were just talking about you."

Me? I almost turned around to see if someone was standing behind me. Why would he, and whoever else was hiding in the house, be discussing me? I was surprised to find out that he knew my name. The only reason I realized that he was Holden's father was because I had seen his picture in the paper once or twice. I tried to force my mind to let go of the fact that Holden was from such a successful family.

"Oh, hi Holden," I mumbled after tiptoeing inside. I had no idea what was going on, but I also had no intention of asking. Go with the flow, pretend you heard nothing, be nice and ask Holden to go out for a soda. This was my plan. Every once in a while I was glad to be a young woman. This was one of those times I could act naive and stupid and no one would question my motive.

"Anna, good to see you," Holden whispered, gently patting my shoulder. I could barely feel his touch, he graced my shirt as though it was on fire.

"Holden," I asked him as though no one could hear me, "what's going on?"

"What's going on here, young lady, is that Holden's mother and myself were having a conversation with our son before you arrived."

"Oh, I'm sorry, really, I didn't know you were going to be discussing family matters. I'm actually not the kind of person to arrive somewhere unexpected...unannounced, I mean."

"You can stop right there, we don't need the whole story. We were working with Holden to get his life in some sort of order, and we will continue with him later on. You're free to do what you will, but I am making it known to you right now, Hannah--"

"Anna--"

"that my wife and I do not approve of this relationship."

Holden's father left the room while I stood shaking. When did this all come about? I was eager to drill Holden, why hadn't he told me of his parents' disapproval before this? I had to be embarrassed to my face, not a chance to prepare a defense.

"It was nice to meet you, Hannah," his mother cautiously smiled to me.

I didn't even care that they had my name incorrect. Nothing mattered to me at that moment. My life with Holden was a fraud.

10

"Anna, listen, can we go somewhere for a while and talk?"

"I guess."

I just wanted to go home and crawl under the covers. Maybe if I slept all night I'd wake up forgetting for a few essential moments that Holden and I did not have what I wanted and expected: profound love, and more than anything, endurance.

We drove to the diner and sat at the booth I used to call ours. Holden urged me to eat dinner, as though nothing major had come down minutes earlier.

"I'm really not hungry, Holden, but please, you order something for yourself."

"Anna."

"What?!"

"Well then, can I get ya somethin' to drink, dear?" the waitress inquired.

"You serve liquor here?"

Holden hid those indigos behind his palms. How odd a smooth-talking man would have callous hands.

"Oh, sorry, I'll just have a chocolate soda."

"Okay, sweetheart."

"Just keep 'em comin'."

"Anna?"

"Yes, Holden!" Boy, did I have an attitude pitched. I felt so foolish and used I figured that I might as well play the game, too.

"Please, can we talk about what happened?"

"I don't have much to say, but if you do, sure, shoot."

"Don't get upset."

"I'm not."

"You are, settle down, please."

"Holden," as always my emotions were my pilot, "what's going on? I love you, I just came to tell you something, I don't even know what now. But, what the hell happened back there? Why didn't you ever tell me your parents didn't like me, and honestly, why don't they? I never did anything to them, did I? I've been good to you, what have you said to them?"

"Anna, hold on. Let me explain one at a time. First of all, I've said nothing but wonderful things about you. They just think that... that..."

"What? That we won't last? That I don't really love you?"

"No."

"What then?"

"That I could do better."

What a harsh response, but I appreciated his truthfulness.

"Do you agree with them?"

"Of course not."

"Well then that's all that matters."

"Anna, listen, I really have nothing to offer you other than my love and my name. *I'm* not rich, and I doubt that I ever will be."

"I know that."

"I know you do, love, but my parents seem to think I'm destined for some outrageous fame and wealth. Even if I could have that I wouldn't want it. God has drawn me to writing, just like He has drawn me to you. Nothing will ever part us, not my parents, your parents, time, distance, nothing. We will be together no matter what. With God's love we are strong enough to overcome anything. Keep believing in us, my dear Anna, if we stay focused on our love, we will be strong. He has empowered us to triumph, and we will. Nothing can break what we protect because no amount of force or dissention can destroy two people in love with God's blessing."

Stunning. Riveting. I've never heard Holden speak with such force and directness. Who knew that underneath his sensitive, gentle skin lived a fighter. We could overcome this adversity, I vowed to not let disbelief ever torment me again.

"We will sow seeds of undying love, fruitfulness of God's grace," I caressed his hand as I licked the air with such words. "We are two united by rusted copper tracks over soft pastures, stopping long enough to pause on the cushion grass and taste the sweet milk."

"Oh, Anna, I love you. You will be an extraordinary writer."

"Uh-uh."

"Sorry," he bashfully conceded. "That's right, you already *are* a writer...May I have your autograph?"

"Funny, you are, but I never turn away from a fan." Jokingly, I penned my signature onto a chapped napkin: Anna Percy.

11

"Miss Anna, there's a card here for you."

"Me?"

"Is that boy mailing letters to your work now?" Elliot asked. "He should realize this is a place of business, not some love fest."

"Oh, Elliot. Give that to me."

I ripped the envelope from his hands and torn deep into it.

"Let's see, let's see," Elliot chimed in attempting to retrieve the contents.

"No! I have to read it first, it might be personal."

"Ooh, personal."

"You guys, come on, I'm serious."

"Very well then, we'll return to our loveless lair!"

"So over-dramatic!"

I sipped each word he wrote slowly, ensuring not a note of passion was ignored.

My Anna,

Like only a wife could, you remind me of all the beauty in life, of which I've seen and much that I haven't. Please endure all that I ask of you, I promise it will not be in vain. Soon this depression will be

40

over and we will begin our lives together, the way God intended it to be. Disregard every word out of my father's mouth, he does not see the spirituality which churns inside the body of romantic love. As for my mother, her heart is her guide, just as yours. She must agree with my father for the sanctity of the family. Yet know that her love is there for you, she blesses us in her own way. You have entered the gate of my heart, a place that no woman has ever been before. We're both on our way to achieving so much, professionally and personally. Like little droplets that took so long to fall, all of our patience and work has joined into a river, which will flood with love in the future.

Still yours, and forever will be,
Holden

"Well, what does it say, Anna?"

"What I already knew. Elliot, please don't think I'm foolish just because I'm young, but this is something special. Something...which few people get to have and I am so grateful to have it now. God has blessed me like I never expected."

"Your cup runneth over?" Elliot teased.

"It has, Elliot. It has."

"You love him and you're certain he loves you...I see it in your eyes. Don't ever let anyone have you believe otherwise. I don't know a lot about this boy, but one thing I do know is how lucky he is. I wish I were in his shoes. No really, it must be amazing to be in such a position, finding the person you've waited for your whole life, and you two haven't even waited that long!"

"Elliot, can I ask you something personal?"

"Sure, you know you can ask me anything, Anna."

"Why are you alone? I mean, you're the kindest person I've ever known. You always look out for me and Carmen and everyone else, like a brother, a father, and a friend all rolled into one. Any girl in the world should be ecstatic to have you. I just don't get it. And I've always wondered too, since I'm on one of my rolls here, why are you so alone, in general? I mean, other than the people here I never see you with anyone. Are you shy or something? I--"

"Shy! Me? Come on, did you forget who you're talking to, hun?"

"What is it then?"

"Really? You want to know?'"

"Yes."

"Anna, I'm gay."

"*What?*" I really wished that I hadn't said that. Elliot didn't need me to overreact during such an honest exchange.

"I'm gay, that's why I'm alone, that's why people in this town despise me, and that's why I've been kind of leery about your boyfriend. He seems like a nice guy and all, but I'm a little, well, let's just say unwelcomed, by his Christian league, if you know what I mean. Understand, he has his right to his opinions, so I won't hold it against him, but I have a right to my life. All I ever wanted was to be treated like a human being. Not an animal, or worse, a criminal. Should God choose to send me to hell for being what I am, I will accept that. But I see Him as being more of a loving God than anything else. Does He hate me? I do not know."

"He doesn't hate you, Elliot. I don't know if he hates what you're doing," *oh sheesh, I gotta way with words,* "I am not going to speak for God. Holden follows the Bible and--"

"I know what the Bible says."

"Listen, sorry. I, I'd better get back to work."

"Yeah, me too. But hey, sweet letter."

"Thanks."

"Cherish it."

"I definitely will."

12

$\mathcal{T}$he proceeding month was truly a time of guided growth for me, thanks to Holden, of course. I was constantly analyzing our relationship, when I was supposed to be working or writing, but I couldn't help it. I wanted to be sure that everything would turn out as it was supposed to.

Holden nourished me in every way, he liberated me from my customary days of self-doubt and indecision. We had declared our love like two Shakespearean teenagers, and promised each other to let no ambiguous elements interfere with our future plans. Only God could have torn us apart. As I was feeling confident by this recurring self-discovery, Holden appeared like the angel he was.

"Holden, what are you doing here?"

"Saying goodbye."

"Again?"

"I'm leaving in the morning to take the train to Des Moines for another conference. Garry said there's a good chance that my book will sell for sure once the economy's a little improved."

Aah, Garry his literary representative had it all figured out. He wasn't a literary agent, just a sweet-talking salesman. I'm certain he told Holden whatever he wanted to hear. Of course, I mentioned none of these thoughts to Holden. I just encouraged him and begged him to come back soon.

"Seven days, love. I'll be back in a week, okay?"

"Okay. Will you write?"

"You know that I will."

At least I had that to look forward to. I treasured Holden's letters. One always finds a way to write unspeakable feelings. We could share so much in our letters that face to face would silence us. I didn't want to be deaf to any emotion, kind or not. In fact, I was rather pleased to learn of his parents' disapproval. Not at first, of course, but after I thought about it I realized that it was better to know the truth than to be lead on with false hopes.

He called me that night before he left and sung an original ballad which he had written only for my ears. While Holden is a master of improvisation, I could tell he stewed on the romantic tune, inserting every bit of heart-felt emotion into his lyrics. He was not established in the writing community yet, but I appreciated his God-given talent. I bet even his parents didn't face him in awe the way that I did. More than anything, I was grateful for his ability to capture passion, revolt, discouragement, spirituality, and obligation into a few simple verses. The fruit of everything he said and wrote was wise beyond his years. I contemplated the secret to such maturity for a man, and how he could remain calm and God-focused during uproars. For the brief span of time we had been together, Holden never faltered. I staggered through life, gripping my faith, clutching all emotion that didn't squeeze through my fingers like soft butter under paced pressure.

That week without Holden drug on. I felt depressingly lonely, realizing that I couldn't talk to my parents, and Carmen and I were too radically different. I couldn't discuss literature and writing with any of them. No one understood. Not even Mary. She had a passion as well, but even I couldn't comprehend the world of dance. It was all very elusive to me. Most of all, she still hadn't had a boyfriend. I know that she wanted to concentrate more on ballet, but there was no possible way that she could fathom my love for Holden. Needless to say, I didn't hold that against her.

Figuring my luck, Daddy was in a terrible mood all week. He had troubles selling his crops, as did most farmers at the time, but I suppose I always brushed him off, expecting him to figure things out as he always had done before. My mother and he stayed up talking all night the day before Holden returned. I could hear them, talking plain as day. I suspect that they thought I was sleeping. Little did they know that I was snuggling in bed with my day's letter from my love.

Anna,

Things are really looking swell for me, for us! God has granted me talent and your love, and I am certain that is all I need to succeed. Soon enough my book will be purchased and I will have enough funds to seriously begin a writing career. Better yet, I will be one step closer to my greatest dream: proposing to you. Goodnight my love. I will see your beautiful face again soon.

Love,

Holden

P.S. I wouldn't recommend a train ride to anyone you know. It was so jolting and uncomfortable that I swore God was sending me a warning to get off. XOXO

Bursting through my door like a tiger out of its cage, Mary belched the highest pitch of a squeal that I had ever heard.

"Anna, Anna," she breathlessly repeated. My adrenaline was pumping furiously through my tired veins. I was so scared at what she came to maliciously announce that I was immobile. Had something happened to Mother? What could it be? Speak, Mary, speak!

"Anna! Did you hear? We're...we're..."

"What, Mary! Spit it out!"

She was obviously hyperventilating, but at the moment I didn't care. I just wanted to know what the hell she was in a tizzy for and what the big news was. I wasn't interested in being calm and nurturing right now to her, I just needed information. I craved for a word to pass her lips.

"We're moving."

"What? No, we're not. Says who?"

"Who do you think? Daddy. I heard him tell Mom downstairs that we have to sell the farm."

"That's ridiculous. Daddy would never sell this farm it's been in our family for too long. Besides, where would we go?"

Thank God for logic.

"I don't know. I heard him say some place to Mom, but I just ran in here to tell you. What about my dancing?"

"Your dancing? You can take that anywhere with you. What about Holden? I can't leave him, I won't. Besides, we've been talking about getting married when he returns from his trip."

"Married?"

"That's right."

"Anna, are you crazy? What about everything you've worked for?"

"Oh, God, not this again from another person. Spare me the lectures, Mary mother of all. I don't need *you* getting on *your* high horse either. Holden and I are fully aware of what we're doing. So, please, don't anyone worry about us, and don't anybody question us! I'm tired of proving and justifying everything to everyone every second of every day. I will be a writer, live with Holden, and go to college. These are three things I am certain of. I am an ambitious person, as you *should* know, so don't doubt me, okay? Please, give me a break. I'll--"

I had been so caught up in my melodrama that I neglected to see Mary sobbing on the corner of my bed. Oh Good Lord, think of all that I had just said.

"Mary, hunny, I'm sorry. I didn't mean to explode in a fit on you. You're terrified, I can tell. I'm so sorry, I know you came to me to be supportive and just give you a big hug, and I didn't. I've let you down. Oh, Mary. Oh, Mary."

I held her gently, patting down her coarse hair.

"I just want to get away, to anywhere. I'd go to the moon right now if I could to get away from this fighting."

"Mary, I know. I hate arguing, everything about it. Don't worry, we'll all be together and everything will be fine."

"Except for you and Holden." She bowed her head, almost in recognition of the pre-death of our relationship.

"No. I won't let that happen."

13

For some strange reason, Mary and I startled our parents. They raced upstairs, wondering to pieces why we were arguing and now hysterically sobbing. Like they needed a response from our mouths instead of their minds.

"Think how your conscience would respond," I thought to say, but as always, I thought twice before I spoke.

"Well," my father waited, "what's goin' on here?"

"Is it true that we're moving?" I questioned; *you're* moving, I thought.

"What in the Good Lord's name are you talkin' about?"

So, Mary had it all wrong.

"Daddy, I heard you tellin' Mama," she spoke up, defending her reputation in a family without one.

"Alright then, girls. Settle down, we'll explain."

My father gave my mother some encoded special look. I take it that this glance signified for her to sugarcoat the bad news we were about to hear.

"There's a moment in all of our lives," she began her political caressing of our ear drums, "when we must move on to wherever God wants us to go. For our family, we need to move on."

"To something better, now that's *moving on*," I insisted. "Us, we're moving down."

My father's lips puckered in anger, but my displeasing remark left him silent.

"Anna," my mother said, "times are hard, we keep telling you girls that, but you don't understand. Now, I don't expect you to, but you have to trust your Daddy and I that we only do what's best for this family at all times. Do you think we want to leave this farm and our home?"

Holding his arm around her shoulder the way that Holden so often comforted me, my father embraced my mourning mother. She was so emotional during any crisis, that I was actually shocked that she made it through her short speech without crying sooner.

What could I do? I couldn't beg them, nor could I fight them. They were like the political system looming overhead, so vast and richly powerful that only a fool would rebel. For some odd reason though, the first in my lifetime, I felt no desire to defend my stand. God could lead us to any land, and Holden would still love me. Nothing would ruin us, regardless of some financial crisis in a country which I didn't even believe in. I felt no patriotic love for America, I was an American because I was born here, no other reason at all. Whatever the money problems were of the moment, which I had to force myself not to diminish, I would not feel insulted by fleeing our home.

"We'll all be together, Anna, Mary, and that's all that really matters."

I said nothing. I walked over to my bed and crawled under the covers. Everyone was still in my room, but I easily fell asleep. I just wanted to see Holden again.

He returned joyfully, excited to tell me his news.

"I found a publisher, Anna. My book will be on the market by... what's wrong?"

For some reason, unbeknownst to me, I lost it at that particular moment. Everything had clustered inside of me for so long that the mere sight of Holden was causing it all to unravel.

"Holden, my father has to sell the land, we're moving to Texas. He's going to work on my uncle's cattle farm until we can get back on our feet again."

It was as simple as that. There was nothing else to say.

"Oh, Anna, here I am rambling on about myself when you've been hurting."

"No, it's okay. Everything will be alright. I just need to know that you will still be there, or here, or wherever you will be, you will still love me."

"I always will. I will love you until the day I die."

"Oh, you shouldn't say that! It creeps me out."

"What? Why!"

"Because I don't like to hear always, forever, never, those kind of words anymore."

"Why not?"

"Because. Do you know how long forever is? Have you *really* thought about it?"

"An eternity. Beyond the end of time."

"Right."

"Yeah. So?"

"I don't want you to tell me that you'll love me *forever,* unless you're certain what it means...everlasting, binding. I'd rather you say, I love you right now...or..."

"Anna, who says that? That's funny, love, that really is."

"*Holden,* I'm serious."

"So am I. Don't you get it yet? I will love you eternally. I mean every word that I say. Nothing will ever change how we feel because this is what God wanted for us. My love for you is as binding as His love for both of us."

Heavenly Father, thank you for this man.

14

We met again at our diner. I had lost count how many times we had sat at that booth and discussed our dreams and fears. He looked directly at me like an arrow to its target. I suspected there was something he wished to tell me, but I didn't force the issue. He had already given me the gift I longed for: his word of endless love. I didn't anticipate anything greater, for God had blessed me enough.

"When do you leave?"

"A week from tomorrow."

"Hmm."

Neither of us had anything to say. It was times like these that caused people to lose their sanity. I bowed my head, staring at the grains of sugar and salt stuck to the wooden table. I wished I had a brimmed hat on, so Holden wouldn't see my fear. How was I to leave him? While I believed that distance could not break us, I had the strange feeling that his notion was not similar.

"You're like a paradox, Anna. One moment you're quiet and contemplative, the next you're flirty and sociable."

"I think we're all paradoxes then."

"You're probably right."

"I suspect so."

"Listen, Anna. I love you. You know this." I nodded. "What

else can I say but we're both still quite young and in a stage of life which does not possess much freedom and independence. We will have to wait, but that suits us just fine, huh? We are used to being patient. All the time we have been apart thus far hasn't hurt us, has it love?"

"No, it has done nothing but make our love stronger."

"See, then? It'll all work itself out. Keep your faith in me, and in God, and I promise you we will survive."

"But, Holden, I want to do more than survive. I want to win."

"I've never heard you so assertive."

"I want to be sure, that's all."

"There's no way to have such certainty, it's all in God's hands now."

"Where it should be."

"Where it should be."

15

$\mathcal{M}$oving day came easier than I had anticipated. We were so busy that there was no time to remind myself of leaving Holden. Plus, the confidence now pumped in my veins. I didn't need blood to survive, only him. As we climbed into our rusty truck my father noticed a wad of paper on the windshield. The corner of what appeared to be a crumpled ball of newspaper loosely hung onto the wiper blade, clinging for its dear life.

"It's for you." He jokingly tossed the garbage onto my lap.

I gently unfolded the paper, a sheet of the Times Daily, which had been perfectly folded into the shape of a rose bud. Inside, a message from Holden. It took me a moment to begin reading it, I was aghast at how a dirty ink sheet could be transformed into such beauty, he never ceased to impress me.

Only one line was tattooed over the machine print: *If you don't know what love is, then I don't know...you're the one who taught me.*

I reconstructed the rose and placed it on top of my bookbag. Holden needed my strength and I would not fail him. At any price, I would juice our love with the nourishment it needed to survive. He was right, if we could sustain ourselves through a few more necessary trials, we would win. Once reunited, the agenda would no longer be complicated. Such love could not be contained. As a realized living being, it could survive life's crude mockery.

Two weeks passed before I received a letter from Holden. I didn't worry though, because I understood how busy he was publishing his first book. He promised me I'd be the first to have a copy in my hands, within six months, he suspected.

I heard from Carmen more often. She strung her run-on sentences together mindfully, attempting to cram every detail of her glory with Alex into a few simple paragraphs. I began to crave home, or what used to be home, but everything seemed out of reach. Daydreaming became my favorite pastime. I scolded myself for not appreciating the time I had in Holden's presence, though I know very well that I did. My parents reminded me that being committed at such a young age wasn't so noble. I wasn't trying to be a martyr, I was living the role God had intended for me. Of course, they still didn't understand, but I didn't bother with them much. My only focus was my writing and my Holden, just like it used to be.

16

Over the next four months I wrote Holden nearly every day. However, no reply was granted. While I worried about him, I didn't worry about us. I knew our strengths, as well as I knew Holden's weaknesses. I decided after torturing my mind for three more days to call Carmen.

After we chit-chatted for ten minutes about charming Alex, I proposed my intended question.

"Do you know why Holden hasn't written me?"

"Um, I'm not sure," she said with a drawl.

"Come on, Carmen, I know you know something. Please tell me. I'm beginning to get really worried. Is something wrong with him? Is he sick?"

"Oh no, Anna. He's fine. Really. He just misses you."

"Yeah, I know, but why is he ignoring me?"

"He's ignoring his heart...He's torn up inside, I heard him talking to Alex about you last week. He couldn't forget you if he tried, but he is trying to--"

"What!"

"No, don't think of it that way. He's hurting so much."

"Yeah, but why doesn't he tell me? We could talk it out like we always did!"

"Things are different now."

"No, they're not. Not between us. He said nothing would change--"

"But things have--"

"No they haven't. I won't settle for that--"

"You may have to--"

"Well, I refuse to believe--"

"Believe what you will, Anna, but you're not *here* anymore. You don't see him. He looked like *hell*, Anna. Hell." I've never heard Carmen cry. I was certain that if anything could make her distressed it had to be serious.

"Just tell him I love him."

"I will. And don't worry, Anna. I know it's easy to say that, but we all deal with new issues differently." She chose her words with precise caution. "For you, you panic and need to tell him, constantly reminding him, that your love is unwavering. For Holden, he retreats and doesn't like to discuss it. It's two different means to the same ending. All that matters is you both love each other and are hanging in there. What more can you do?"

"Tell him I miss him."

"I will, Anna. Take care of yourself."

"I love you, Carmen."

"I love you, too, intrepid girl."

17

Two more achingly long months passed until I again heard from Holden. He sent me a copy of his first novel, the science fiction book that he had been working on for nearly three years. I barely glimpsed the title, <u>Crimson Jet</u>, as I rushed to the dedication page. I was dying to see my name in print. Nothing. A sweet line to his mother and father, for their 'love and inspiration,' but nothing more. I tried to not let it bother me, but it did. We both promised to dedicate our first books to each other. Had he forgotten? Or perhaps, promises weren't worth as much to others as they were to me. Still, I was overcome with raw emotion to receive something, anything, from Holden. Oh, how I still loved him dearly. Not a single second passed when I swore I hadn't thought about him. Since the moment we met he has been the tenant of my mind, I sold him the space just as land is sold. The only difference was that it was not my doing to give him my thoughts, but God's. He insisted for me to love a man, who at times was reclusive and difficult, but I never loved him any less. Absence does make the heart grow fonder, it is so true, I don't care if it's cliché now. I can understand detesting such phrases though, Mary keeps cheering me on like some obsessive go-getter, 'out of sight, out of mind.' I refuse to repeat such crap. Like physical presence has anything at all to do with love. The only thing that mattered to me was that *eventually* we would be together. I mailed

Holden a letter the following morning, thanking him for the gift and praising him for his work, I had stayed up all night reading the book. I'm sure Holden was having lingering thoughts of the possible failure of our relationship, but I was not. And this too was evident. I replied so eagerly to his letters. Too forceful, too earnest? I had no idea, but I refused at this point to be something that I was not. Holden had loved me before for whom I really was, so I had no intention of putting on any airs. In fact, he always adored that I was ambitious and expressive. I would not change unless he directly asked me to.

Wouldn't you know that two weeks later he did. He sent me a small, simple, but very sweet card. I could tell that he made it himself. Inside, he wrote of a few new happenings. At the bottom he simply put, "I miss you." Nothing more was written, except for one afterthought: *Anna, you do not have to write me every day. Goodness, I received three letters from you one day last week. I know you miss me, but I am alright.*

I did not know whether I should be insulted or at ease with such a comment. What was wrong with writing every day, every moment, if it helped me to feel closer to him? I had to express how I felt. I, unlike Holden, could not pretend to move on with my life. Such overwhelming panic sunk in, that I ran to my mother recounting every detail. I insisted that I had to see Holden.

18

My mother drove me back to our real hometown. I thought that I would feel nervous to be in such a place where I no longer belonged, but I didn't. The moment we arrived within the city limits I began to feel better. Now that I was home, I could see Holden and Carmen and Elliot again. I knew exactly what I wanted to say, too. Holden could go his own way if he wanted to, but I was going to fight for him. I did not care, nor hesitate at all, that it could cost me some dignity. I would tell him the truth and then just enjoy every waking second we could have together. My mother advised me to keep our meeting brief if it wasn't going well, so I promised I would. She spent the afternoon with old friends, while I showed up on Holden's doorstep. His mother answered the door, to my dismay, yet she seemed extremely pleased to see me.

"I'm sorry to show up unannounced again, you must think that I have no manners, but I absolutely must see Holden."

"Come in, Anna. I'll get him right away."

She smiled at me and embraced my shoulder. I had never felt such affection from his family. I was nearly to tears already, when I noticed Holden standing behind her. I had not one minute to react, he leaped towards me and hugged me as tightly as he ever had. My chest was constricted, but I did not care. We stood in the center of his living room, physically closer than we had ever been before. I stopped holding him, but he didn't let go. His thick arms were still encircled around me, his fists pushing into my spine. I still hadn't seen his face, it rested on my left shoulder. His mother had come and gone from the room, but more footsteps entered. His father, I suspected. Yet, Holden still wouldn't let me go. I stared straight into his father's eyes, for he was standing immediately behind Holden. He glared at me, but in an odd manner. I wasn't sure what to make of it, but I quickly reminded myself that it did not matter. Holden was back, the man that I knew, loved, and missed. In one brief, yet vital moment, I regained my confidence and he showed our love to his parents. It was the most stunning display of emotion, from a man who prided himself on never touching a woman. The days of sitting nervously at the diner, his forefinger lightly caressing my chin, like a sliver of wind, were over. This was the moment of ecstasy I had begged God for.

The words exchanged between us that afternoon are the most precious words I have ever heard.

"Do you know how much I love you? How I've longed for you, and yet been terrified that I've lost you?" My desperation pounded his tender heart. "Holden, please, don't ever leave me again."

"Anna, I've never left you. I love you, I'm just scared that I'll sit here wasting away, loving a woman that I'll never be with."

I wanted to fight this point, but I didn't. I'm not quite sure why. I think I just wanted to enjoy our time together. It was better than it ever had been. We sat outside his house, on the velvet lime grass. I stared at him and he blushed, his boyishness had remained here though I had not.

"Come here," he grabbed my arm and yanked me next to him. I practically fell atop his lap. I expected him to say something brilliant, as always, but instead he kissed me and I thought how disturbing it was that I'd forgotten the softness of his lips.

"Do you know how long I've waited to do that for?"

"Nearly six months?" He laughed at my literal ways. No, I hadn't changed either. While some people, myself included, often craved change, it was nice to see that Holden and I were exactly the same... except for the emotional scars. While I sat thinking these things, I felt his eyes upon me. I looked up and waited for another kiss, or perhaps a silly comment.

"You know we're getting married, don't you?"

I couldn't think of what to say. Literally I was mute. Holden had informed me of this before, but never with such confidence. My fate was sealed. God had spoken and we had answered.

"Thank God for our love, Holden."

"He said you're welcome."

I'll remember this day, and how perfect it was. We ate dinner with his parents and Alex and Carmen visited over coffee afterwards. I could not thank my mother enough for returning me to where I belonged all this time. We could only be absent from my father's presence for a couple of days, so it burned me to tell Holden we would part again so soon after reuniting. He had grown quite well to understanding external circumstances. I hadn't even realized how proud I was of Holden. The man he had become and every day further defined, was more astounding than the boyish writer whose rhetoric yanked my ankles off the ground that day we met...the final day that I was a child.

19

*G*ood Lord, I'm so high strung I can't sit still. My head aches as much as my heart used to. Have you ever felt like you were running sideways in a dream, and you couldn't quite figure out why everyone else walked in a different direction? This is worse than envisioning myself naked, clumsy, *and* speechless in front of a group of strangers. I wonder how God determines when we've had enough misery and it's time for happiness now. Possibly all of our spirits are marked with some sort of destroy date. When our time has come to spill the vicious poisons from our body, it will be done. If God chose happiness for Holden and I, at this instant it would be granted.

Yet, I don't want to dismiss that none of the outcome lies in the boundaries of our control. We all decide our own level of indifference, thus passing on blame to everyone but ourselves. Still, I can't help but wonder if a time will ever come when Holden and I will be united in a physical sense, the way we are now spiritually and whole-heartedly. Let me review my options, as though they have changed. You see, it's like the lawn in front of your house. You must take care of it yourself. Perhaps you're a bit lazy and the sky waters it for you. But what happens when it does not rain and you still neglect your duty? Your lawn will gradually die. If you're lucky enough, you'll realize the sad scenario sooner rather than later and you'll mend your apathetic ways to save the grass from death. But, again, what if you do not? Who do you have to blame? Simplified it sounds, I know, but love is very much the same as that trampled grass in front of your porch, which, to your surprise, is quite fragile under the worst of circumstances. Can love be saved no matter what you do? Probably not. Holden and I will continue to persevere, but I cannot help myself, I wonder who is to blame if it fails. God? Holden and I? Whichever the louse of us decides to call it off? These are the ramparts of my mind. Like any other woman in love, I am slightly crazy. I have odd fetishes like I never used to, and greater than anyone has noticed, my self-control and common sense have been off more than on. No, personality is not a light switch. But then again, neither is love. I cannot turn off my feelings anymore than you could make yourself honest if you are a liar. Who we all truly are is up to God, or *was* up to God a long time ago. I just hope He understands what He has gotten my heart into.

20

After muting my inner demons upon returning home, I reflected more sweetly upon my blissful hours with Holden. He telephoned me the weekend after our hasty return, just to remind me that I was not forgotten. No, I was not glutton for punishment, this would not be another one of those occasions when my hopes rode up a golden elevator, and shot down when my karma kicked in. I would no longer force my relationship to live in a glass house, for God had planned something so extraordinary for Holden and I, that if anything cursed me, it was my lack of trust in *Him*. I should have known better.

It was around this time anyway that I began to focus more on risk-taking for the sake of what I referred to as 'my certain future.' Elliot and Paul needlessly reminded me that no future was certain, as though my brain had shrunk overnight and I no longer had an ounce of logic left within me. My realism had not disappeared, I just forced it to hide behind my new-founded optimism. Whoever believes that something is doomed will discover how quite brilliant he is. I would not tempt fate to betray me. I grew to prefer my now relic belief: love exists as a gift more than a thought. I had already obtained Holden's love, now I only needed to sneak into his lifestyle.

"Hello?"

"Sweetheart, I had to hear your voice again."

"Holden!" Quite right, he telephoned me the following Saturday as well. "It's so wonderful to hear you again. I've missed you so much!"

"I miss you too, love. You know what I truly miss?"

"Hmm?"

"Kissing the cream off your lips." What? This didn't sound like something Holden would say. But then again, I am *practically* the man's wife.

"Uh-huh."

"So, have you done any more writing?" he asked.

"Yes, of course. I'm working on a piece now about a doctor who can heal thousands of people's bodies, but can't do one thing for his own soul. Only on his death bed does he accept the truth that a successful man could be such a failure to God."

"Interesting notion."

"Thanks. Anyway, Mama and I visited the university here and she's pushing me into the writing program there."

"Is it a good program?" Holden always wanted whatever was best for me.

"Oh, I think so. It doesn't matter, I'm returning to Kansas for school."

"You are?"

"Oh yes, I'm certain. Do you think I could take four more years away from you?"

"Anna, you have to do what's right for you. I don't want to interfere with your life?"

"Not interfere with my life? You only own my heart. It's a bit late for--"

"I didn't mean it like that. I just want you to have the greatest chance of becoming a writer." Why did people have to always elude to my gender? I prayed that someday we would not have to be so conscious every second of what sexual beings we were. "But...it would mean everything to me if you came home."

"I'll be there. Don't you worry. I'm on my way home."

Everything changed after that conversation. Now that I saw a way out of Texas, and a road back to Holden, I was determined more than I ever had been in my life.

Though my life was quite complicated the rest of that year, my love with Holden seemed very simple. I didn't overanalyze us, or really even analyze us at all. I concluded that if I rode out the time left in Texas, I would be rewarded for my patience. Everyday I continued writing Holden a little note. It was almost like he was an imaginary being, like a character out of a book with once I had been infatuated. So out of reach, as though in the presence of his being I would giggle and point like a disbelieving child. I knew both of my parents, especially my father, would be ridiculously disappointed in my returning to Kansas, but I allowed myself to be selfish. That, however, I do not regret. It was my life and sooner or later I had to live it for myself.

"I'm moving back to Kansas," I announced, spooning lumpy rice pudding.

"You think so, huh?" Boy, my father was quick.

"Yes." I would not argue, I had been doing well that entire year choosing my battles cleverly.

"You're going to throw you entire future away...No. I won't do it. I won't argue either. You think you can walk on into this kitchen, proclaim your little information, and then smugly turn away? Fine then. So can I. You want to go? Go. Drop the subject...Now, Mary, how was your recital?"

Finally. I had shouted enough that someone finally heard. I felt victorious like I just conquered my greatest challenge: my father.

"That sure was easy," I thought, guaranteeing myself that the worst was over.

Love made me stupid. Not foolish nor confused. Stupid. I still don't believe I deserved the end result, but God must have. Free me from that proceeding hell, I begged. He turned away. And soon after, Holden followed.

He was right. He always followed in God's footsteps.

21

$\mathcal{I}$ cannot disclose when exactly Holden and I broke up. I don't even know myself. Basically, I figure he'll let me know the rhyme and reason when he concludes that the decision involved me.

You see, I drove myself all the way back to Kansas (strangely enough, he himself never made the trek) to inform Holden face to face that I would not be moving within his reach. After attempting numerous times to call him or write him a paced letter to share the grim news, I decided that he needed to see my eyes when he heard it.

My father was right. I had thrown everything away. Any scholarship offer, every possible chance of attending college, in order to *try* to be with the man I loved. It did not matter now how well I had performed in secondary school, nor that I was voted Most Likely to Succeed. What was done was done. I had given up security for a chance, only a chance, to be with Holden. Still, I cannot say that I wish that I hadn't.

"Why did you do it?" Carmen asked. I stopped by the library before punching the truth to Holden.

"Carmen, what do you think is the worst fate a person could have? To be grotesquely ugly, lonely and depressed, or perhaps poor and hungry?"

"To be hated," she replied.

"No, no. This is much worse than that."

"I don't think so."

"It is."

"Fine, then. I would say that nothing could be worse than feeling alone in the world."

"Wrong. See, as horrible as it is to feel alone, sad, miserable, hungry, weak, whatever, nothing is worse than having regrets. I truly believe that. Yes, because I'm foolish and an idiotic romantic, I will die lonely and penniless, but I will die with a clear conscience, unlike most people I know. Come on, how many people do you think really can say they regret nothing?"

"Very few," Elliot whispered to himself.

"At least I tried."

My journey continued that day to visit the only man I have ever loved. What should have been another perfect moment was cut short by the truth bubbling on my tongue. I don't know where I got the strength to say it all, but thank God I did.

"Holden...I found out that I will not be moving here because all of my money wasn't enough to bring me to school in Kansas and it's really screwed everything else up in my life, but I don't care. I know I will survive and my words will live on in my writing, all I wanted to do was tell you face to face how much I love you, and that I regret nothing at all. I would still to this day trade in everything I own and every small scrap of hope I have to be with you. I love you so much, and I just hope that you don't forget me if I can't be here to hold your hand, kiss you on your birthday, laugh at the jokes in your books written only for me...I swear I will never love you any less than I have, and I know that means gigantic proportions because the love we've shared for the short time we've had together has been more true and pure and unconditional than what most good people receive and give in a lifetime." I had said it all, regardless of the fact that I stared at the buttercups on the ground the entire time. I had lost my pride over the strain of that year.

He said nothing. Nothing. Was he in shock? Did I need to get a nurse? My God, I understand it's a blow, but speak! Speak! I needed him too dammit, and inside his little mind he was counting the consequences upon him. Had I let him down? Of course, he loved me and I didn't keep my fucking promises.

I stood in the field alone. Yeah, he had long since headed back to the barn. Milk some sympathy from the cows, I thought. I'll talk to the crows and tear out your buttercups. I did, too.

$\mathcal{M}$y greatest dilemma to date: how would I supply myself with enough love to get over Holden? There could be no greater love possible than the unconditional, eternal, *yet overrated,* love that I had for him. Oh, I swear, if I could have made myself stop loving him, I would have. How dare he deny me so little as a response. You know, it's funny how some people will walk away as though nothing had ever transpired.

Paul took the piss-smelling bus to come visit me. He was really the only person I kept in contact with, including those who lived a bedroom over, because I didn't have to pretend around him. I was pure misery at its sourest form. Paul could relate.

"See, Anna, it's like I said, love does not exist for everybody. People spitting their pretentious words at me, 'oh, there's someone for everyone. God has a special somebody in mind for you!' Please, it's all a hoax. God doesn't even give people food, shelter, basic health, why the hell would he give everyone romantic love? It's absurd that anyone would even think that. Morons."

"Pff. You've got that right."

We slouched on the concrete steps, ignoring the pains in our backs and the heat which pulsated through our skin. Fry me alive, God, I dare you.

Over Paul's three day stay, I called Holden seven times. Not once did I say anything though. I just wanted to see if he was home, or if he was maybe by some odd chance on his way to Texas. He answered five times though, so it was pretty much hopeless that he had any intention of patching things up.

The day after Paul left I uprooted every flower in my mother's garden. I knew she'd be angry, but I didn't care. What was she going to do to me that would make my life worse? The only beauty of the madness, was that I became untouchable. My soul was dead and my heart was with a man who didn't want it, there was nothing God could do to hurt me anymore.

I also buried the cross Holden had given me. My father was gleaming, more than when I graduated high school.

"You've gotten your brain back, baby," he said.

"I'd rather have my heart than my brain, but fortunately for me, my choices have already been made. There's nothing I want to be granted but privacy and permission for shallow thoughts."

My father walked away in disgust. No, he hadn't won me back either. I was out of reach now to *any* man: physically, emotionally, spiritually. For all I cared, my father, Holden, and God could cruise over to some Pacific Island and laugh about my naive ways. If I believed that I controlled anything, it was my reaction to situations. I would never allow another man to rape my heart like Holden did.

"How can you utter such words?" Mary questioned. She was too innocent for her own good. But I did miss those days myself.

"I love him still."

"It doesn't sound like it."

"To you, maybe."

"You have all these wisecracks and stupid remarks to defend yourself from the real truth."

Mary, Mary, quite the little detective now. Airs aside, she was right. I knew it, but what did it all matter? As long as I was passing through this passage of insane passion and misery, I would have to accept this fraud of a life.

23

The truth was that our love benefited Holden enormously, but he neglected to respond with gratitude. I still loved how old fashioned he was in his high morals and development, so brisk with unsung emotions and iron-clad commitment. If a woman's heart is a tower, mine is the cheesecloth-manufactured building, teetering at the push of the weak breeze or a bird's foot, so dark and ghostly empty, needing a bulldoze more than a junkie needs a hit.

Sure, love, strip me of my basic need, your affection. Why don't you just challenge me to a nice round of quadratic equations. I would have had a better chance of succeeding, or at minimum not being squashed by a cynically sexless man.

Ruth once echoed to Naomi, 'wherever you go, I will go,' so the same between Holden and me. I continued to write him honey-soaked letters. Though my resentment and acidic anger preoccupied my swinging responses, I expressed my devotion to Holden as lyrically as customary.

So many months passed with no reply that I lost count. Actually, I probably could have shot off the exact number but I didn't want to be reminded. We had been apart nearly as long as we had been together. How odd it is that two slices of time could feel radically different in length, though they were nearly precise to the day. See, there are many things that most of us cannot comprehend. One of them, is goodbye.

For hours at a time, I would float on my bed, lying awake thinking what Holden was doing that moment. Sleeping peacefully, no doubt. He was always a sound sleeper. I was ashamed of myself that I not only had grown accustomed to my sleep disorder, but to my eating and mental ones as well. How could so much evil come out of what used to be good? Not just good, perfect. The greatest gift God had ever given me had quite equivocally ruined my life. I wonder if he knew that. [He implying God *or* Holden.]

Needless to say, my writing flourished during this time. Misery is the best motivator for anything. Don't be fooled by what you're often told to dismiss: sadness is not pathetic. If anything, it is genius. By God, I had genius, and I would not deny it anymore.

No longer did I distinguish amongst the little specialties of life. The variations of seasons, the taste of peppermint ice cream or a salty bagel, the smell of roses. Yet, for some odd fantasy, I would sit outside on our ratty, poor excuse of a lawn, flickering away the floods of bugs mounting my pasty white thighs, smelling the newspaper rose Holden had made me. To a complete stranger, or a sane person at that, it was bare of odor. To me, the pleasantness of things past, passed the days like delusions couldn't.

And as if destiny hadn't done enough, we were able to return to our farm in Carson City, where I belonged all along. I wanted to track down Holden, just to catch a glimpse of his crooked smile, but I discovered upon my less than illustrious arrival that he too was gone. Off to bigger and better things, being the writer I always knew he'd be. I was tempted to grill Carmen for details, but I wouldn't do it. Elliot was kind enough to hire me back, regardless of the hardships he faced economically. Although I was home, I felt out of place.

24

ecause we so often question God's motivation for the resulting mess of our lives, I will not attempt to impress anyone with my doing this. Could it be that I had misinterpreted what He intended for me to do, love Holden that is, and now was stuck in some middle life that He could not rescue me from any better than I could rescue myself? It was the same question as always.

I tried to force myself not to keep track of Holden. I really fouled up and sent him a birthday card that year, and oddly enough, he responded. Just a brief thank you, for remembering him. Did he honestly think that I could forget the man I had intended to marry? No girl ever forgets such a thing. Besides the fact that I find human beings to be quite unforgettable, unlike some flaky movie or cake recipe, and other than God himself, no one occupied more of my being.

"Do you realize you have a love-hate relationship with God?" Paul asked of me on what would have been my anniversary with Holden.

"I do?"

"Yes. You either blame Him for everything that's gone wrong or you love Him like a preacher would."

"Hmm." I didn't know quite how to respond to such an accusation. Paul usually didn't say something so profound to me unless he really believed in what he was saying. "You really mean that, don't you?"

"I'm serious, Anna. There's something wrong with your logic. I mean, you used to be one of the smartest, *most* logical people that I knew, but ever since you met Holden, and had your *whatever* with him, you really lost that."

"How sad."

"It is. Now that I think about it, it honestly is a loss."

"I don't mean to blame Him. If anything, I should thank Him for staying with me after Holden dismissed me. It's odd, isn't it, what we think to be love is not, and what we forget to be love, is? All this time, I've focused on Holden, who in reality doesn't love me, but I've forgotten God so frequently, and yet...He sincerely loves me."

"Everything about love is ass-backwards, I'm convinced."

"Yeah, you're right. Besides, people may love us without making our hearts flutter."

"Does that matter so much?"

"It shouldn't, Paul. But it does. I miss feeling the way I used to. With Holden, a light turned on inside of me. My body was warm, my soul tanned. There was something so savvy about getting away with that much love. Like it was illegal, or at best, unnecessary to love at that level. You could have thrown me into a desert with nothing for shelter or food and I would have died happy. But now... now God has given me an abundance of time that I cannot use, Paul. What's the point in having a massive forest to yourself if all you know how to build is a train? I could love until the ends of the earth, when God's milk dried out of the breast of every mother, but I will not be given that chance. Do you understand? My gift, my talent, is not writing, nor logic, nor compassion, it lies in my ability to love. And my gift, to God's dismay, though also His approval, *will* be wasted. I guarantee you that."

25

There are moments in everyone's life when we feel utter abandonment, though God has closed His gates to us and we must create our own safe haven. My moment came two months after confessing to Paul that I could have died happy had God kept Holden near to me. My mother always told me that a man would never make me happy unless I was that way already, but I disagreed. I recant my earlier statement, she was right. She loved my father dearly, I know, but even having experienced profound love did not ease her death. Instead she died happily, knowing God's love foremost and crying out to Him like a babe aching for a parent's touch. Or at least that's what Martin Magus, the grocer, told us about her death.

She was struck by an auto on her way to the pharmacy, but needless to say, this did not kill her. What did was so vicious and displeasing to the eye that Martin and Marian Magus fled Carson City after viewing her bleeding corpse on the dirty street. Martin said that mother stopped inside his rick-rack store to borrow a carving knife. I'm not quite sure why she would since she was supposed to pick up some medicine and return home, but this circumstance will never be sorted out. Anyway, she asked to borrow the knife and return it the following afternoon, which Martin permitted. Of course, Mama has a fine set of knives, but who was Martin to know this information? She left with the object, crossed into the street, was struck by a car, thrusting the knife into her abdomen, ending her life within two minutes.

Unfortunately, no one was around to help her other than the Maguses, which is remarkably odd for it was the busiest alley in the city, but who am I to argue with the man's story. As the daughter of the deceased, I could do nothing more than grieve.

This event changed my life more than any other, including all of my tumult with Holden. I appreciated life in a new regard, realizing the precious value of loving each moment. Is it a sin to love a man without his approval? I didn't care. In my eyes, the only wrong I committed was giving up on love. What if Holden and I were limited in our time left on this earth? It terrified me to think that we were wasting days frolicking around for a better match. Although Holden had made his decision, I was going to change his mind. I swore on my mother's grave, that the only wall that would barrier my reaching Holden would be what God alone would create. I begged Him to allow me another opportunity to express my devotion and use my gift.

I swarmed Holden with letters and poems urging him to contact me. After three weeks without a reply, I begged Carmen to convince him to see me the following weekend. Finally, I had a plan.

26

$\mathcal{H}$olden did pass the weekend at Carmen's, visiting with his brother and someday-future-sister-in-law. I, however, did not get to enjoy his company. There was little else that Carmen had to say to me about the uneventful event, except one important factor.

"I wasn't even going to tell you, but--"

"But--"

"But, he did ask about you."

"He did!? What did he say?"

"He just wanted to know how you were."

"Oh like, casual conversation, or was he really wondering?"

"Anna, don't do this again."

"Do what?"

"You know exactly what you do to yourself. It won't get you anywhere, you know that by now, right?"

"Yes, I know. I mean nothing to him. It's long over. Blah blah blah. Just give an old friend something sweet to fantasize about, okay?"

"Fine. He was very sincere. He wanted to know how you were, what you had written, if you worked at the library now that you're home. The usual sort of stuff anyone would ask."

"Did he ask about--"

"No! He did not ask about your personal life, so don't even get started."

"Okay, God! Well, how did he say it?"

"I'm not doing this run through with you, Anna. Goodbye."

"Wait, please. Don't hang up. I just want to know if I still have a chance."

"I thought you insisted that you *never* had a chance."

"I'm past that really. Come on, Carmen, please? He owns my heart."

She sighed. We sat in silence, neither wanting to speak the unpleasant truth.

"Anna, I think he loves you, he always had. But that doesn't matter. It's over."

"It matters to me."

"Don't get all upset. I'm sorry, I didn't mean it that way and you know it. We can't always be with whom we love, even if they desperately love us back."

"Why not? I *still* don't understand that."

"See, you like what you can figure out. You and Holden are both that way. But love isn't a game or a puzzle, it's intangible, like a lifeform unto itself...Alex describes it more as an alien," she chuckled. "Oh, I don't know, Anna, just quit doing this to yourself. You could find a great guy if...Look, I know you don't want to move on and you're having trouble letting go, but just quit pretending. It won't happen again. Not with Holden anyway, alright?"

"Yeh."

"You alright?"

"Yeh."

"Anna!"

"I gotta go. Thanks."

There really is nothing that compares to living your life, loving someone from afar. Such loneliness. At night I hear my father rocking in my mother's old creaky wooden chair, tapping his fingernails on the side they way she used to. I can't imagine that level of seclusion. Me, I sit in the bathroom on the cold waxed floor.

27

So much time has passed since Holden and I were together, but I still feel the same. My emotions are slightly more extreme (between ravenous and numb), but I love him no less. In fact, I've continued to nourish the spirit created between us. It burns me to say that it resides in my heart, for it's in the total plasma of my being. I don't miss him, I long for him. I'm not saddened, I am heartless. I am not bitter, I am biologically altered, now incapable of loving another man regardless of my will. Even though I've expressed my unconditional devotion to Holden using every means I know, nothing places me into his attention range.

I try to believe what Paul said, that if Holden loved me as he insisted, and as I loved him, then we would be together now. I did everything I could, more than perhaps I should have, and still our spirit failed.

"Are you going to Carmen's wedding?" Paul asked me that afternoon, knowing I didn't want to discuss it.

"Paul, I *said* I don't know."

"Anna, you have to go, Carmen's one of your best friends. Besides, you shouldn't punish her for inviting Holden."

How could I not go? Carmen stood patiently by me through all of my mess with Holden. I knew it would be torture seeing him again, but what I feared most was being trapped in my own imagination.

"I'm not scared of seeing him." Paul looked at me with utter disbelief. "No! I'm not...what I'm scared of is seeing him and falling in love all over again."

"What difference does that make? You're still pining over him now."

"Aargh!"

"I know, I know what you're saying. I've felt the same about Lanna. You'll be thinking about him missing you, and you'll cautiously walk into the church, expecting miracles and nothing happens, when just then--poof! he'll pick you up and kiss you...no, better yet, he'll be on his knees begging for you to come back to him. He'll brush your hair from your face and say 'Anna, I've loved you all this time...Thank you, oh God, thank you Anna for waiting!'"

It was frightening how well Paul knew me. I was ashamed of myself, but the hope just wouldn't die no matter what I tried to force myself to believe. Heart over head, always with me.

"That's it," I muttered. "I already fantasize about Holden too much. If I see him again, and he smiles at me, I'll be worse off than I am now. I'm barely surviving, Paul."

Cue my nervous breakdown. This was the fate I never envisioned, but dreaded the most. Would we meet again, and would he want me back? Being dumped on a whim was tormenting, but face-to-face conflict would crush me.

"I won't live past that night if he denies me."

"I know," Paul whispered, his eyes grimly closed.

"Hi, Carmen, this is Anna. Oh, good. Um, Paul and I will be able to come to the ceremony and reception. I'm sorry it took me so long to get back with you...I-I'd be thrilled to go. Okay, see you. Bye."

It was too late now. I would have to face Holden again. One may think that I would be a stronger person for countering my trials, but with Holden, I was as weak as an ice cube in the desert.

"Anna, you look beautiful. He's going to drop dead when he sees what a knockout he gave up. Good thing we'll be at a church!"

I'd been struggling not to cry all morning, but the droplets punched through my face, tearing the color right off my cheeks. I was in too much agony to laugh for Paul's sake.

"Be strong, Ann. Get yourself together. You've survived this far: *Sorrow is better than laughter: for by the sadness of the countenance the heart is made better.*" I looked at the heart-shaped face in the mirror, too aware that this visage was my only heart left.

"Anna, I know how hard this is."

"No, it's okay. I'm in so much pain now that there's nothing anyone can do to hurt me anymore. I've killed my grace and compassion, and brainwashed the romantic optimist right out of my soul. I don't know the man I'll be seeing today, he's obviously not the loyal, sacrificial person I once knew."

"Maybe you never knew him at all...Sorry, that was a cruel thing to say."

"I've heard worse. Anyway, who knows anymore, it may be true. I just need to keep reminding my conscious that Holden never existed."

"How are you going to do that when he's right in front of your face? Come on, Anna, you can do better than that!"

"Thank you, Paul, but I can't. Holden and I are strangers. I'll greet him in the same manner as I do all the other guests. Unless, of course, he comes to me first." My face lit up any time I thought of us back together.

"Anna,...*don't.*"

The church was beautiful. I chuckled to see the flood of white lilies (Carmen jumped overboard decorating). Nevertheless, it was calming to see her touch.

"It's now or never, Anna."

Paul clutched my hand. My body shook in fear. He attempted to hide it by grabbing me like some sort of conductor, but people already were staring. Carmen's mother, a nurse, spotted me, her eyes diagnosing my affliction. I stopped shaking, my body trying to defend me from any attention-getting devices.

"Hello, Holden." I jumped behind Paul, hoping again to make myself disappear. There were no words to express the flutter of pain and love twisted into the fate of that moment. Holden. My Holden. There he was in a crowd of people, admirers I'm sure. Smiling and carefree, swiping his blond hair from his forehead. I wanted to run up to him and see his sweet blues light up. Oh, just to be a part of his life, even an admirer in the crowd. That's all I wanted.

"Anna, go say hello, you know you want to."

"Oh my God, I don't know if I can, Paul."

"Anna! So glad you came." Great, it was Carmen's mother popping up. She was charismatic like Carmen but she talked so loud I feared Holden would look over. Yet, for as bubbly as Mrs. Hensen was, she was also very perceptive. "He looks so handsome, honey. But you are a sight to be seen. Turn around for me! Oh, goodness, you're so lovely, tiny like a little china doll."

"I want to say hello to him, but I'm trapped in this moment. I feel like I need to learn how to walk again--"

"Anna--"

"Oh, Mrs. Hensen, do you believe that love always finds a way?"

"No, Anna. I don't." I had never heard her use such a serious tone. My limp mouth waited for her explanation, but fate instead provided one.

He kissed her. If I thought my pain level had a threshold, I was wrong. My knees buckled, stomach knotted, and tongue shriveled. Thank God the wooden pew broke my fall. Mrs. Hensen tried to catch me, but the stunning look on her face took a few seconds too long to react to.

"Anna, sweetheart, are you alright?"

"Alright? No! I'm not alright." I cried, shrieked, talked, and gasped all at once. Paul tightly enveloped my shoulders with his arm and led me to Carmen's dressing area. It only made me more nauseous to see her lily-white gown. I should have worn that dress. I should have married Holden. Only I never had the damn chance.

"A chance!" I shouted. "All I wanted was a chance!"

Mrs. Hensen put her cloth-embroidered handkerchief close to my mouth, to muzzle the screams, I'm sure.

"You saw her." Even on her own wedding day Carmen was a wonderful friend.

"Don't tell me anything about her. I don't want to even hear her name, I'll *hate it* forever. How old is she? She looks like a child. Let me guess, the perfect Christian girl, a step up from me. Do you *think* she loves him the way I do?"

"Anna! Settle down." Paul was right. I had to get a grip on myself.

"Carmen," I cried, "I'm so sorry. I won't make a scene. This is *your* day. I'm so sorry. I'm so--"

"Shh, it's okay, Anna. I'd react the same. Just try to relax. Paul, take her and sit on my side of the church where she won't be able to see him."

"Thanks, Carmen. You deserve such beauty."

As I left her room, I wondered why some of us were destined for love while others were meant to be alone.

"God."

"Hmm?"

"It was God."

"Where?" Paul smirked at his own wit. "You *are* in his house."

"No, I'm serious. Why did God have me love Holden, knowing Holden wouldn't love me back?"

"Anna, come on, this isn't the time for philosophy."

"No, wait. Hand me that paper over there." I dug through my purse for a pencil. Somewhere inside of me, a messenger was talking. I wrote every word quickly and precisely:

After all of these years, I've finally concluded my theory on life itself. We are all passengers on a train. Some of us enjoy the ride, looking out the window, gazing into the eyes of strangers, as though we prefer not to be in control. Then, there are the rest of us, myself included. My stomach twists and turns at the thoughts of all that I don't control in my own life. Why should I even refer to it as my own? It isn't, it belongs to someone else. Perhaps God, perhaps not. I care not to discuss semantics right now. For this isn't a story of theology, it is one of love. But, if God is the conductor of the train of life, please tell Him to pull the fucking thing over, I'm getting off.

For a brief moment I felt better. I needed to blame someone, anyone. Love was the most overrated and unfair existent. I realized how cruel and quick-tempered I had been with the people in my life. I was tired of seeing people in love, while I was endlessly and needlessly tortured. I crumpled my writing into my tiny bag and walked with Paul into the sanctuary.

I carved a path directly to an open pew. Forcing myself to not acknowledge Holden was disgusting. I never wanted to revert to the childish antics he had sold his soul for. We were seated just as the organist began the processional. I dazed off a couple of times during the ceremony, not wanting to hear the vows of undying love ringing in my ears. During a couple of moments, I sensed a jabbering of weakness and had to glance at my message. I could no longer cease the force of temptation. Holden and the mystery woman feigned ecstasy, pure love in its falsest form. He continued glancing at me, almost too-obviously, as though he would have shouted at me from across the room had he had the chance.

Just as I was saying a prayer in my mind, for no reason that I could comprehend a startling sound burst from the sanctuary doors.

"Stay seated and shut up!"

Three men wearing plaid shirts, navy pants, hiking boots, and face masks shouted orders from the center aisle. Two of them had shotguns, the third stood by looking anxious and confused. These men were not the professional thieves that the newspaper depicted blistering the surrounding cities with high-staked burglary. Still, it was evident that they weren't quite sane enough to avoid a trigger-pulling flinch.

"Look, ain't nobody gonna get hurt if y'all just stay seated and listen to me. Alex, over here, pronto. You know what we want."

There were only about a hundred people present, it was a fairly small church. Yet, the men came to the right place if they were searching for cash. Alex's family was loaded and everybody in the state knew it. It didn't take a genius to map this one out, the wedding announcements were printed in every paper: state, city, even in the high school paper's community news section. I remained calm because I figured they'd take some cash and flee. The police would be called and reports would be filed, but otherwise it was still a wedding. There was no way Carmen would be upstaged, even by criminals. I loved that about her.

"Hey!"

A gun went off. I whiplashed my neck straining to see what happened. Of course, someone had to try to be the hero, I suspected. Every crowd has a few. By now half of Alex's family was discussing terms with the conversational thief. There must have been some sort of problem, either dispensing the cash or the rich clan decided not to part with it. It was apparent the criminals were tired of talking. The leader ordered everyone back to his or her seats, and Alex to retreat to the altar. Something was brewing that was crossing another line of danger. I trust my instincts in every situation, and I knew that this crime had moved past the stage of being a grab-and-run robbery.

"You! Here!" Holden. He grabbed Holden. I wasn't really surprised that he knew who Holden was, because his picture was often in the paper when a story on his parents or superstar brother was published. Why would he take Holden hostage?! He didn't have any money. God, don't let this be some twisted ransom deal! I swear those never turn out positively. "Let's go guys...This one's comin' with us. When you have the money rounded up; be ready. We'll contact you in two hours."

Someone had to do something, Holden wouldn't be brought back alive, I could feel it. Before any of us had reaction time, the men were dragging Holden down the aisle by the collar of his suit jacket.

My love for Holden kicked in. Instinctively, my heart reacted. I knew that he was still first in my heart, without stopping to think about any risks.

"Why are you taking him?" I asked the leader.

"What?" He stared down at me, shocked that a woman would ask such a stupid question.

"Why would you take him? He could beat you up if he had the chance. Look at him, he's a strong guy, trust me. Plus, if you take someone from a high-profile, uh, well-known family, all the cops in the county will be on your tail in ten minutes flat."

"Is that so, missy?"

"Yeah, it is." I stood up. "Take me." I was staring fearlessly into the eyes of this tormented man. I barely noticed Holden's disgusted and shocked face.

"You?!"

"Yeah, I can't defend myself against any of you."

"What's in it for you?"

"Nothing." I paused and settled on Holden's image. I wanted to remember him, in case they decided to take him anyway.

"Fine. Let's go."

He let go of Holden, pushing him onto the lap of Carmen's father. For a moment, I was scared. What had I done? I had gotten myself into another situation I would not be able to escape. I started to pray when a stranger from three pews behind me flew out of nowhere and slammed down one of the armed thieves. I could live still. What would Holden say to me then? Perhaps in his near-death experience he would have discovered his suppressed love for me. What happened next was too fast to conceptualize.

"Anna!" I was on the red carpet, Carmen gripping my hand.

"Somebody call an ambulance!"

"Anna!"

"Paul, step aside, let my mother help, she's a nurse."

"Oh God, do something! Save her!"

"Paul, please, step aside."

"The exit wound is torn ragged. I can't stop any of the bleeding."

"Mom, she's not conscious. Do something!"

"There's nothing we can do sweetheart, she's gone."

"Look at her!" Paul scolded Holden. "She's dead. *Now* will you look at her?!...Where do you think you're going?"

"Paul, let him go."

"No, Carmen, he needs to quit running. I've got to catch up to him. He needs to own up to the pain he caused Anna. Oh Lord, I can't run this fast. Help me...Where the hell is he going? Holden! Stop!"

"I can't," cried Holden to himself. "I've got to catch that train."

28

Holden boarded the train, an impermanent escape, but Paul was able to proclaim his final glorified message.

"Holden, do you hear me? I know you do! Holden...she said she'd die for you and she meant it. Do you hear me? She meant it!... Holden, *she loved you, you owe her! You owe her!*"

"God...please, forgive me. I am so sorry. Oh God, I am so sorry. I, I, I never meant to hurt her. I loved her. I did. I did what you wanted of me, but I got scared. What else could I do but push her away, it was wrong, I know that now but I couldn't love her, if I could have I would have, but only time could have...no, nothing could have helped, it was me who wasn't good enough, not her, not Anna, not my dear sweet Anna, I'm so sorry, sorry Lord, forgive me and hold her close to you, love her as I never could, never did, but wish now so much that I would have, oh if I could do it all over, I would, I swear God save a special place up there for me to be with her, my angel, my Anna. I'm sorry, I loved you so."

The quartet played the same song as on Holden's last trip home to see Anna.

> *I am bleeding, but I have felt love*
> *Destined for pain, I escaped it because of you...*
> *You brought me a perfect love so pure and real*
> *You taught me how to feel*

Without you now, my heart will never heal...
I love you, but don't deserve you
You've gone to a better place
On every angel I dream of
I will see your beautiful face.
You were a gift from God
I'd do anything to get back
And I'm sorry now, I let you down
But you had everything that I lacked.
You gave me...what I didn't have
You loved me, but now I am sad, and the tears will flow,
with no place to go
Down my face...
I will smile, you're in a better place
I loved you, didn't deserve you
You've gone on to a better place
On every angel, I will dream of...
I will see your beautiful face.

Part Two:

Jonathan & Cora

1

$\mathcal{I}$ learned about life before I lived it. That's what Cora always says, anyway. People tell me that I should have thoughts of my own, and cease to constantly quote my girlfriend, but, what can I say, she has wiser thoughts.

Cora and I met during a time of my life which I care not to remember. I was riding the rails between Kansas City and Rincon, New Mexico. The Atchison, Topeka and Santa Fe Railroad Company was booming in business and, because of this, busting at the seams with passengers, many of which were broke twenty-somethings like me. I was terrified at first of riding the rails, but nowhere near as terrified as when I encountered Cora.

She stood before me dressed in all white; an intricate lace dress which dusted the floor and enveloped her delicate frame. Her hair was neatly smoothed back and tied with a white ribbon. She looked angelic, pure, nearly-flawless. I remember instantly wanting to touch her skin because of the lack of imperfections and the abundance of fair, creamy tones. I could feel, simply by looking, the softness one would encounter in caressing her face.

"Jonathan, Cora. Cora, Jonathan."

"Hi," I uttered.

"Why hello," she said with the easiest smile. I expected her lips must taste like honey for the sweetness in her grin.

"I thought it would be interesting to introduce you two," Pavel chuckled.

"What's so funny?" I annoyingly uttered, glaring at Pavel for mocking my worthiness to occupy the same space as the striking Cora.

"Nothing," he murmured between giggles. "Well, have fun getting to know each other!"

Pavel bustled away, still snickering delightfully in his quick exit.

I turned to Cora, afraid to approach her with my nervous words and revealing temper, and stated pointedly, "well, I'm sure there's a reason why he introduced us."

She stood calmly, still smiling easily at me and holding her hands gently together. The pause carried on for at least a minute and then, finally, she responded.

"He introduced us because I asked him to."

"Oh," I whispered.

"You see," she began, "I was grumbling on again and again about how difficult it's been for me to meet someone, a male you know, and Pavel had this odd idea that we could perhaps be suitable for one another and so he suggested I stop up here today and since it was a lovely day and all, I thought I'd give it a go, so--"

This was a remarkable moment. I saw her vulnerability now and it entranced me. She seemed so fragile and childlike when she spoke and I realized her poise did her too much justice. Women like this were exceedingly rare; so cautious to be exposed, and so respectful too, but eager within their eyes to be connected to and under the protection of a man.

"So you came. And here we are." I smiled broadly, and my confidence returned.

I requested Cora to take a walk with me, through the faint downtown of Holten, about thirty miles north of Topeka. I wanted to get away from the city for a little while anyway and I was eager to have her company for the ride there and back. She agreed, needing only "two seconds" to be ready which, naturally, turned into twenty minutes. I minded little because it provided me a moment to catch up with Pavel and instruct him on the wisdom of my ways.

"Oh, please, Jonathan, give me a break." I enjoyed witnessing Pavel's eye-rolling now. "Ok, so big deal. She asked to meet you. You've met. And now you're dragging her up the road to a town in the middle of nowhere so you can witness her being car-sick and bored with your history lesson on the Potawatami Reservation. Wow."

"Say what you'd like, my friend. But that woman will be mine."

I rushed back to the spot outside where Cora and I had agreed to meet. I expected that I was far ahead of her readiness for departure, but the thought of her searching through passers-by for me horrified my soul. Rightfully so, I waited another seven or eight minutes for her, not minding one bit. When she emerged from the ladies' room she looked more radiant and refreshed than when I had met her minutes prior. I did not consider it possible that she could be even more beautiful, but she was.

"Hello again." The fluidity of her words was like a melody in my ears. I prayed she would talk the full ride to Holton so her captivity over me would ensue.

"Hello, Cora." I reached out for her hand and she offered it immediately. I was tempted to squeeze it tightly, except for my fear that I would damage the tiny bones. "Are you ready, my beauty?"

Her smile widened. "Yes!" she replied. Her eagerness forced me to question within my own mind if she had ever been complimented before.

During our trip I was distracted by my own foolish thoughts. Well, they were good ones actually…like how had this lovely young woman remained unattached? And why did she seem so alone and neglected in compliments and respects? I only declare such thoughts foolish because they were tugging my attention away from her.

"So, where exactly are we headed?" she requested.

"Well, I thought we could walk through downtown Holton, maybe along New York Avenue, over to 7th Street."

"Why? What's in that direction?"

"Rafters Park."

"Oh…Have you been there before?"

I debated how to answer her question. *Hurry and think of a reply, Jonathan, you don't have all day…*

"Yes. I have."

"Hm."

Thank goodness that was all she said. A simple "hm."

She continued to look intense in thought but still had the easy smile aboard her gentle face.

"And when were you there?"

I knew it. She's crushing me with the follow-up question. *Think, think, think…*

"Oh, fairly recently."

"That's a funny answer," she snickered.

"Why is it funny?" I said, nearly offended.

"Because what may be fairly recent to you could be ancient history to me."

"Oh." She had me there. "I'd say it was about a month ago."

"Ah. See that wasn't so hard, was it?" She smiled broadly again and my heart skipped a beat. I felt like I was melting as she took her hand in achingly slow motion and placed it on top of mine. She held it still for a couple of minutes and I could feel the coldness in her slender, weightless fingers. Yet, I was so lost in amazement of her decision to do this that I didn't relish the moment as I should have. She reached her hand away and laid it back onto her lap like she was placing a rich, cloth napkin atop her upper thighs in preparation for a State dinner.

All the while I was struggling to remain a gentleman and not stare at her with an iota of lust.

"Cora, what do you enjoy doing?" I choked the words out to say something. She looked at me with slight bewilderment; I'm sure she was wondering why I was nearly faint.

"What's wrong? Is something the matter?" The concern in her voice was intoxicating.

"Nothing…Is it warm in here?" The beads of sweat sat motionless on my forehead and around my collar. It was the start of my developing a heat rash, too, and my throat was as parched as Jack Perrin's in "The Phantom of the Desert."

"Yes," she giggled. I knew she was covering for my embarrassment.

"You are adoringly cute." I couldn't resist uttering it.

But there was no reply. *You are a fool.*

"Cora, I apologize. Please, continue, and tell me about your interests."

"Continue? I hadn't started, Jonathan." Then, she was silent.

So this is where things take a turn for the worse, I thought.

2

Fortunately, eventually our car stopped and we exited for fresh air and further awkwardness. Rafters Park was both splendidly scenic and overwhelmingly dreary at the same time. On one side laid sprawling grass, horseshoe pits, and the populated ball diamonds. Across, hovering just over the edge of Elkhorn Lake stood a massive Bur Oak tree; the kind you would see lightning strike in a terror film. Cora and I strolled through the park as though it was the English countryside and we were Heathcliff and Catherine.

In the distance I observed a couple cars bumping down the gravel of Kansas Avenue and I thought once more of my historical travels. Really, I wasn't a pursuer of the culture and exhilaration that led most people to exploration, I was a highway hobo and there really was no sense in hiding that from Cora. Suddenly, I felt rather depressed.

From the look on her face I realized that she was enjoying herself so I attempted to cloak my gloominess for merely the time being. Predictably, Cora was exquisite in her stroll; her face glowed from the sunlight atop it and her hair bounced ever-so slightly from the gentle breeze. She enveloped her hand around my elbow and I felt her trust of me deep within my bones. We were unremitting in our walk and I lectured myself to savor every moment as it came. We paused near the oak tree and, despite my childish fear of it, I suggested we sit briefly.

It was surprisingly chilly under the tree and I wondered if I should be concerned for Cora's warmth. I hesitated, however, out of fear of appearing foolish since I had just insisted upon our rest. *Ask her if she's cold.*

Minutes passed and neither of us said a word. Cora still held that day-dreaming look on her face as though she had not a heed in the world, or the remembrance of my company. I could think of nothing to do, nothing to say.

The clouds drifted quickly overhead and I guessed the shapes as if God was molding them for our whimsical entertainment. Every now and then I glimpsed over at Cora from the corner of my eye. Her eyes were upon the landscape and not me so I persisted in sparing her of my disturbance. I suppose because of the tranquility of our surroundings I too became lost within my imagination and, without premeditation, I began to sing.

I rode Southern I rode L and MN,
I rode Southern I rode L and MN,
And the way I've been treated
I'm goin' to ride the rails again.
The way I've been treated sometimes I wish I was dead
The way I've been treated sometimes I wish I was dead
'Cause I've got no place
To lay my weary head.
I rode—

"What is that you're singing?" Cora broke her silence.

"Oh, it's a Merle Lovell song about riding the rails." I let out a nervous laugh and then paused. I had no idea what Cora must think of me now.

"Well, keep going!" she cheered in her own sing-song voice.

I cleared my throat and inhaled a few breaths. *Relax, she's already heard you sing.* So, I continued.

I rode Southern I rode L and MN
I rode Southern I rode L and MN
And the longest one I've ever rode
It is now began.
I'm a ramblin' man, I ramble from town to town
I'm a ramblin' man, I ramble from town to town
Been lookin' for two blue eyes
And now they been found.
I gave her my watch, and I gave her my chain
I gave her my watch, and I gave her my chain
I gave her all I had
Before she let me change her name.

We sat still and the lyrics hung in the air.
"I liked it," Cora said.
"Thanks."
More silence. We are obviously good at that.
"Where did you learn that song?"
"When I was riding all over the place."
"Oh yeah? Like from where to where?"
"Well I was in Texas for a while."
"Texas!"
She sounded surprised as though the state doesn't permit visitors.
"Yes, Texas." I smiled. I couldn't help it, everything Cora said was precious to me.
"Oh, well I've always wanted to go there. Tell me all about it."
This was truly the first time a young lady had ever been interested in my life and my journeys. I immediately eased my demeanor and decided to be fond of the interest from Cora.

"Well, I've been a few places in Texas," I bragged. "Paris, Gainesville, Honey Grove, what-have-you."

"Uh-huh, and?"

Wow, what an attentive woman. Now this is every man's desire, I thought.

"Gainesville was quite interesting. The oil boom has just started down there and some people are actually making a decent living at it which, of course, is a relief after the Depression. Probably the neatest thing, though, is the community circus which travels all over the place in Texas and other areas."

"Really?" she giggled.

"Yes." I was unremitting in sharing my vast expertise. Honestly, my ego took over. "You see, Cora, they need jobs and training centers in parts of Texas and the only way to make that happen is to have the population to support such things. It probably sounds pretty funny to say that the circus is bringing in more people, but, you know, it kinda is."

"Oh…"

"Yeah, so anyway, like I was saying, I was there and I also jumped the tracks to Paris."

"Paris, Texas. That sounds funny."

"Sure," I delighted in her naivety.

"What did you do while in Paris?"

"Oh I thought I was just passing through, to begin with, but then I stayed in town for a week or two to see what-all they had to offer."

"Tremendous. You've really done a lot already in your life, Jonathan."

"Yeah," I gabbed away not devoting much thought to Cora's responses. "It's a significant railroad center in Paris, even though you've never heard of it. A bunch of the tracks, the Texas and Pacific, the Midland, part of the Santa Fe, the Colorado, they all pass through Paris. So there's a lot to see, is what I'm saying. It was just a little enticing to me, if you know what I mean, to stay there and all, because they just opened a huge junior college."

"I didn't realize you were thinking of attending school."

Why did she ask that, I wondered. *Does she think I am dim-witted or something?*

"Jonathan?" she articulated to catch my attention.

"I don't know," I muttered coldly. "I guess I was thinking of going."

"Well, why didn't you then?" she graciously inquired.

"Gee, I don't know Cora," my sarcasm smacked her in the face. "Maybe because I didn't even have a home address and, oh, colleges consider that a bit of a necessity if you know what I mean."

As this turn caught us off guard, we both paused from speaking.

Finally, Cora said, "I'm sorry." And that was all.

Twenty minutes passed and Cora arose to her feet and began brushing off her skirt with her hands, despite the fact that there was nothing on it. She quickly glanced at me and I took that as my sign to follow her lead. I stood up and departed from the shade of the tree and the cool of the solid ground. We each took a mere step or two and, just then, I had to say something.

"Wait!" I imposed. "Cora, listen, I'm sorry about my attitude. I don't mean to act annoyed or condescending to your comments. I am really interested in you. And it would just crush me if you dismissed me because I have a dark past."

"I have darkness in my past too," she said matter-of-factly.

I found such a thought difficult to grasp and believe, but decided that I must take her at her word.

"I did not know. I apologize. I want to hear everything about you, Cora."

"Maybe someday, Jonathan. But it's not something of which I like to discuss."

"Alright," I conceded.

And, we left.

3

$\mathcal{A}$fter the complexity of the day at Rafters Park, I planned for a more relaxed visit with Cora the following weekend. Part of me was uncertain of her coming, as we seemed to end our previous get-together on a sour note. But just as I approached Carmen's Café I witnessed striking Cora chatting away with Pavel.

She was dressed in a light pink shirt dress with a thick belt affixed snugly around her petite waist. The outfit completed with wrist-length gloves, polished shoes, and the kind of cloche hat that could pass at church as well as in the jazz clubs. I was amazed at her ingenuity in pulling together good-looking apparel, especially since I was aware of her lack of funds. Pavel leaned his shoulder onto the cream bricks of the café and folded his arms firmly within each other. He stared intently at Cora as she smiled bubbly and talked with a visible spring in her step. Just as I began my approach down the sidewalk, Pavel hurriedly entered the café and returned with two cream sodas. He flung one to Cora and turned his attention to Carmen's daughter, Lisa. He obviously was interested in courting Lisa and, from what was apparent, the fondness was reciprocated.

I stood behind Cora, peering down at her lovely hair and inhaling the familiar strawberry smell of her shampoo. Had she not pirouetted around I would have remained much longer.

"Hi, Jonathan!" Her faced beamed and instantly matched the

color of her dress. I had never seen Cora smile so infinitely before. Every perfectly-white tooth was revealed and her cheeks and lips were flush, cherry, sunkissed.

"Hi, doll. So good to see you!" Today I was giving the swank act a go.

"You too. Cream soda?" She motioned towards the door of the Café, implying for us to purchase another bottle for myself. But this was no longer my style, I decided.

I snatched the soda from Cora's feeble hand and chugged away relentlessly. She looked surprised and impressed simultaneously and her awe recharged my ego. I slurped the last gulp I desired down my throat, wiped my lips half-heartedly with my sleeve cuff, and jerked the bottle back into Cora's hand. Eerily she peered at the half-empty container and then snuck her eyes back up to my face. She grinned with a sort of sexuality unexpected of such a virtuous woman, and I realized then what Cora was looking for.

Delighted in my display of masculinity I then determined to take Cora alone to talk. I tenderly reached for her hand, both to guide her walk and to reassure her of my still-gentlemanly nature. We toddled through the doors of Carmen's and I was instantly thrown back by the dimness and cigarette smoke. Normally such an environment fails to bother me, but with today being crisp and bright in the warmth of the sun I could not subject Cora to said bleakness.

"Let's grab a couple drinks and head outside to the patio," I insisted.

"Ok," she swiftly submitted.

I purchased two root beers and boysenberry tarts and eased through the side door with Cora; the patio was secluded and Cora opted for a small, metal table with two nearby chairs for us. It was uncomfortable and rusty but, because of its dainty scale I knew Cora found it charming. I stuffed my backside into the seat and sensed butterflies swarming within my stomach. Cora impatiently nabbed a bite of the tarts.

"Ooh, delicious," she delighted. "Take a bite."

I didn't think that I could.

"Maybe in a bit, love," I replied.

"So," she stated.

"So," I replied.

Cora giggled. *Damn, she is cute in everything she does.*

"Well, whaddya want to talk about?" she said, still giggling away.

"You."

"Jonathan, be serious!" The chuckles slid through between her words.

"I am."

"No, you're not." But she knew that I was.

"Are you amused that I want to talk about you?" This compelled Cora to pause from sipping her root beer and fiddling with the tart to reflect.

"Sure, I am. I mean…I guess so."

"I suppose you want to know why I am so interested in discussing the great Cora."

More giggles.

"Yeah," she whispered.

"Because I am falling in love with you."

I felt Cora swallow hard and then she began to nibble at her fingernails. Her thrill to my statement was fully transparent and I assumed she yearned to provide me an equivalent reply.

"You can say something, Cora." Now I was the one with the giggles.

"I love you too," she rushed through the words as though they had been choking her throat for ages.

It spoke to the wholesomeness and sweet adolescence of Cora that she would grant such a response. She obviously had glossed over the falling in love phase and headed straight for a lifetime commitment.

I stared at her with delight and wonder until she finally responded again.

"What?" She was actually taken aback.

"Nothing, hon." I smiled, thus, freeing her from anxiety. It was imperative that Cora realized that there would be no concerns on her sweet mind, should she choose me. *She already has.*

"Well, what about Cora do you wish to discuss?" She delighted—giggles and all—in her ability to proclaim herself in the third person.

"Cora, I want us to have no secrets, nothing between us at all. Not ever. Tell me about this darkness in your past. It's something we can share. Anything that bonds us in terms of our similar experiences will only prove to strengthen the trust and commitment that we share. I--"

"Um, remember…I said I cared not to discuss that?"

Cora immediately withdrew. But I couldn't refrain, this was far too important.

"Cora, please, we need to know each other through and through. Love isn't about just presenting forth the good side of yourself."

"Of course," she said omnisciently.

"Well then, what is it that happened? You know, I am willing to tell you anything about myself; I want you to do the same."

"Ok, so then tell me something about you that I don't know." Her sarcasm was thick, almost stifling.

I figured I would oblige her derision and play along.

"You know I've lived all over, right?"

She nodded.

"Well, when I was in New Mexico--"

"When was this?" she snapped.

"Um, about two years ago--"

"Ok. Continue."

"So, I was in New Mexico," *at this point I am completely thrown off,* "and I stayed in a couple different places, Socorro, Rincon... my mind is drawing blank on the rest. Uh, anyway, it was a rough experience--"

"How so?" *Geez, wouldn't she let me get through the story without pressure?*

"In Rincon, the train tracks divide the town in every way imaginable...color, income, lifestyle; pretty much everything you can think of, you know?"

"Uh-huh."

"And I was on the side of the tracks that, let's say, just wasn't so desirable."

"Right."

"I can't even describe how I felt."

"Try." Cora smiled and I felt duty-bound to unlock myself to her and share this story. After all, I wanted reciprocity here. I returned her grin and said, "Ok."

I continued.

"It's one of those things that I think unless it happens to you directly you can never quite get your arms around it."

"I've been judged," she simply stated. "Everyone has in one way or another."

"I suppose that's true." My tension was alleviated and I thought of an unambiguous story to help her understand. "There was this one time when I was waiting for the next train and here stood this upper-aged businessman. He looked me over, up and down, and glared at me disappointedly. He didn't know the first thing about me, couldn't stop glowering for one second to say 'good day' even. He adjusted the brim of his derby hat, repeatedly straightened his tie and smoothed his suit collar. Never for a moment did he stop peering at me. He didn't stare inconspicuously either. He looked dead on into my own eyes, man to man, as if to say 'who the hell are you kid; you don't belong here.' Each time I so much as blinked he reached for his back pocket, I guess to protect his wallet, like I was gonna jump the old man! The thing that got me about it was that Rincon is poor, I mean, *really* poor. It's all Indians and new Mexicans and don't nobody have any money! It was just a little incident, I could tell you much worse you know, but it got to me—like out of all these people, I was immediately spotted and labeled a robber. I've never hurt or challenged anyone. Even a broke fool like me can have morals."

"Aw, I know it!" Cora's immediate sadness stirred me. Maybe she could do more than throw smiles at me; she could understand, better still, she could even relate! *What if all I ever wanted was right before my eyes?*

"I am just so sorry," her words soaked into my ego.

"Thanks," I quickly brushed my hair away from my forehead and looked down at the table. I'm sure I was blushing; even so little from Cora could do that for me.

We gulped down our remaining root beer and I couldn't help but fiddle at the tart. It no longer looked appealing, just dry and crumbled and worsened yet as I dissected it with Cora's used fork.

"It *was* good," she chuckled.

"I bet it was," I flirted. "I'll try it another time."

"K."

Hold her hand.

I cleared my throat and motioned awkwardly, catching Cora off guard.

"You ok," she asked.

"Yes. Ready to go?"

"Of course."

She arose, flattening her dress back to perfection. I abruptly stood and waited ineptly—yes, I startled myself at my own lack of nerve.

It was difficult to touch such a pristine woman, you wouldn't understand.

4

*A*fter taking Cora home I stopped worrying so much about the proper number of days to wait to call her for another rendezvous. We were rapidly growing closer and I suppose I just expected at this point that we were well-suited. The intimacy continued, not more than two days later.

"Hey, you!" Cora exploded through the train station doors into my stiff arms. Before I realized it I was hoisting her ninety-pound frame in mid-air and spinning us both like the Jakobsson duo who won figure skating gold at the Olympics.

Sliding her down my frame, back to the earth, I clumsily joked, "Well we missed the debut Winter games but, hey, maybe we can get in on pairs skating next time around."

She *actually* giggled.

"What's the plan today?"

"Well, Cora, take my hand and I will guide you through this depot brimming with mystery and suspense."

"Ah, you are an excellent host already, monsieur!"

She tightly gripped my hand and I was intent on not letting go. Relaxed, we strolled through the station and I indicated trifle points of interest to Cora. She seemed curious about the Westside Circle and Topeka Rapid Transit lines, but, then again, maybe she feigns interest well. Clearly, pressuring Cora on profound topics was not wise; I had already attempted that and humiliated myself. This time, I objected to merely sustain fine conversation.

"There are a lot of young people in the station today," she whispered to me.

"Uh-huh." *Should I give her a truthful response?* "Cora, they live here, many of them do."

"Oh." She gazed off in bewilderment. "How so?"

"Well, there's still no jobs, you know that, right?"

"Yes."

"See, a lot of those people, especially single gents of course, just ride the rails for something to do, a place to sleep, and, maybe just maybe, the miracle of a better life."

"Hmm."

"Yeah, there are millions of folks with no work right about now in this country and thousands of them are young guns like us and there ain't no way the companies can keep all of us off the rails." I laughed with discomfort. *Not that this is funny.* "I do have to say though that, yup, I've known a few young men killed for trespassing or 'cause of injuries too. I'd see 'em jumping off the rails to avoid getting had and, you may not think that train is goin' fast, but it is."

"I'm really sorry, Jonathan." The unadulterated apologetics in her voice soothed my still-burning wounds. "I can't imagine what you have been through."

"It's really been hard-hitting, Cora." I scuffed the floors flippantly as I dragged my feet; the exhaustion in my soul perpetually apparent. "Hoover with his reconstruction money has kept the railroads going at least, but who can blame us for catching a free ride? He's using the money, *our* money, on businesses not people."

"True. But he can't pay for both…both businesses and social services, I mean."

"I suppose that's spot on. People just don't know what it's like though. I didn't enjoy ridin' all over God's dry country just to maybe have a place to hang my hat or the off-chance I'd find work, which by-the-way I never did."

"I can certainly understand that," she empathized. "I wasn't trying to sound callous or disagreeable. I feel for you, indeed, I do." Cora reached for my hand and crept her cool, weightless fingers in between mine. In that moment, I wanted to cry. I had never been soothed before by anyone, not even my own mother. Cora's knack of enveloping me with love and peace was extraordinary. I choked the tears back as any decent man would, but they came anyway. I failed in disguising my pain, and as my vision blurred with the flood of worthless, watery memories, Cora traced the droplets down my cheek and with her trembling index finger, erased them altogether.

"Can you see the love I have for you?" she said.

"Yes," I murmured. "Cora, I love you, too."

"I know," she simpered. "Good."

We sauntered, hand-in-hand, through the rest of the depot like an elderly couple shuffling their Sunday away in a park. There could be nothing better than this, I knew.

"So did you ever catch a train on the fly?" Cora inquired.

"I can't believe you know about that!"

"Well, why not?!"

Together we laughed boisterously and caught the attention of surrounding passersby.

"Because that's not something with which a classy young lady is usually familiar!" Kidding with Cora was as pleasurable as eating ice cream on a hot summer day, all the while soaking one's feet in white sands or chill lake water.

"Well, did you?!"

"Yeah, I've got trains on the fly before." Perhaps my adventurous nature would tickle her fancy.

"What was it like?"

"It was frightening, Cora." What could I say, bravery probably would impress the girl.

"Ohhh." *Yeah, she's in awe.*

"I would seek out my box car and hop aboard before slippin' under the wheels. It was like grabbing onto a hot plate some days; clutching the steel catwalk and slinking atop a box or freight car, whichever. The main thing is you didn't want to get caught or to drop your gunny sack, 'cause then you'd be out of luck and starving."

"What would you have on you to eat?"

"Usually sardines or some type of bread, maybe with peanut butter."

"Oh. Uh-huh."

"Yeah. So, anyway then, I'd get lucky on occasion and perhaps come across a sparse car or even some canvas to use as a blanket. At night--" Just then I realized Cora was weeping, and attempting poorly to veil it. Her hand shook as it brimmed above her glassy eyes and I felt her urgent desire to be somewhere, anywhere, else.

She sniffled repeatedly, and I prepared a thought.

"Cora, I'm sorry…I see that I've upset you…I didn't mean to and I think we should never discuss these happenings again."

"No, it's okay," she responded as she attempted to compose herself.

"No, really, please. Let me drop the issue, and ask for your acceptance of my apology."

"Truly, Jonathan, it's okay, I--"

"No, please--"

"No! It's alright, Jonathan!" Cora's shouting startled other visitors, not to mention me. Her lips slightly parted, then paused, as she inhaled deeply a warm, substantial breath. I waited motionless and silent until Cora continued on, this time in a voice of femininity. "Jonathan," she cleared her throat, "listen, I too don't wish for you to think that there are things that must remain unspoken. Let's share it all. Let's be open. And let us bring out of each other the good, the bad, the joyous, the painful, the truth, and the secrets."

"Agreed" was the only response needed. And so I said it.

"There is something else that I want to say," she began.

"Yes?"

"Well, there's something I want to tell you, but I've waited until the right time. And I think that this is it."

I was keenly ready, eager for Cora to at last reveal her dark secret. Nothing inside of me felt nervous because I anticipated a trivial event that, to me, would have been easy-peasy but, to Cora, was earth-shattering.

"Go right ahead, my dear," I stated in simplicity and near fool-heartedness.

"A number of years ago, some, not many, I joined a Ladies of the Chorus group at my church and they had such an abundance of members that they ended up branching off the younger ones into a Young Ladies of the Chorus, if you will--"

"Mmm-hmm." *Yes, this was all very interesting,* I appeased.

"So anyway…we got together every other week or so and would rehearse a cappella numbers to perform for bazaars, Christmas services, family nights, what-have-you. At first, it was great fun, despite the hours and the additional tasks we'd be lured in to do as well," she giggled nervously, "and I enjoyed much of it."

"Right."

"But then, as the men's choruses grew too Pastor Davis decided to split their membership into a men's and young men's, respectively." I nodded, wondering if the secret was that she skipped a church chorus practice or if she and the gals spied on the young men during their sessions. "Anyway, we'd perform together—the young ladies and the young men—whenever we could find a good tune and event. It was enjoyable as well and, I suppose it was time for us to get to know each other appropriately."

God, please refrain me from laughing.

She continued, "One particular Sunday I received a post note to attend a picnic at the home of Margaret Carson...She sort-of oversaw the young ladies group...And I thought, 'sure, why not go,' so I marked it on my datebook and headed out a couple weeks later. When I arrived it was quite nice, I admit, with plenty of seating and linen-covered serving tables outside. Just a simple affair but the food certainly looked spectacular...fried dumplings, fresh fruit spreads, Mrs. Carson's home-canned greens, rhubarb pie, buttermilk-soaked chicken--"

"Whoa, there! You're makin' me hungry," I kidded.

We momentarily laughed and then Cora persisted in her lovely tale.

"Yes we ate plenty and drank plenty too—just lemonades and soda punch!—and others played simple games, sang, walked, and chattered away."

"Sounds real nice."

"Yeah, it was; or it should have been."

Just then Cora's demeanor instantly changed, as though the room was flooded with icy waters, darkness, and ghosts. My heart sank and my stomach...it was in knots. I couldn't get the words out.

"You're probably wondering what went wrong," she rescued me in her response.

"Mm-Huh."

"Well, one of the young men from the chorus, Jeremy, was there and he was jovial and could talk nineteen to the dozen. He gabbed away with one of my chorus mates, Lynn, probably because everyone wanted to talk with her, and then he called over his buddy Tony to join in the mix...Tony and Jeremy looked like the two most all-American farm boys you can imagine: churchgoing, hard-working, clean cut, and charming. I just stood there and took pleasure in the conversations as Jeremy facilitated them all. I suppose several moments passed and then Jeremy said 'Cora, you know what,

Tony's interested in writing too, young lady…So how 'bout that!' Jeremy smiled away, self-impressed with his ability to make facile connections. I replied and addressed Tony, saying something along the lines of 'how delightful' and 'I'd love to see your work sometime.' He reciprocated in kindness and enthusiasm, and then invited me to view his work. I was impressed, to say the least, that he carried his writings with him; surely a sign of his commitment to the craft. So we walked into Mrs. Carson's and she was prepping for second servings in the kitchen. Tony enlightened her that he was about to reveal his work to me and she encouraged him to do so. I found it comforting that she lit up at his mention of it and, since I thought so highly of her opinion, I considered it unlikely that anything disdainful could occur."

Cora paused and breathed again and I debated whether to touch her hand or speak a word. Before I decided, she went on.

"So we walked into a side room, presumably a guest bedroom, and Tony opened a leather satchel to retrieve his paperwork. I was busy watching his hands and the bag so I missed his eyes upon me. Before I knew it, he knocked me to the floor and his six-foot thin, but athletic, frame was on top of me. His strong, bony knees were pinning down my arms and his hips crushed my ribcage so it was difficult to breathe, impossible to scream. In two short moves he had my dress up and my undergarments down and he, he, you know, entered me. It was painful because it was my first time but I was too numb to even be bothered by the ache. I can't say that I so much as twitched or wept beyond that point because I knew it was over. He had it, what I had longed to save."

Jesus, God.

Silence. Nothing said could make this alright.

Silence. Saying it was difficult enough. I made her relive it for my own selfish purposes: so I could feel more secure as a man for knowing my own woman through and through.

Silence. *Because I am so fucking angry, I want to find this guy and tear him apart, limb by limb.*

Just then, Cora looked up and stared me straight in the eye. Only two tears had fallen, one solitarily down each cheek. She wiped them away vehemently and re-postured her shoulders and neck.

"Jonathan. Thank you for listening to my story. I don't know what else to say about it other than it was one of the most difficult experiences of my life for obvious reasons, and it adversely affectedly me in so many ways...But I am glad that I told you; you needed to know. Please just keep it in the back of your mind. I don't need to discuss it, but if I ever do, it'll be with you, guaranteed." She smiled brightly and I was amazed by her poise and still-evident compassionate nature. I saw hurt within her, but no anger really. Could she disguise it that well, or, perhaps, she chose to not allow it to consume her. *What a wonderful soul.*

We sat again in pure silence; only the bustling of the depot's visitors and passengers adding background resonance to conciliate us. I permitted time to pass to reassure Cora that I was thinking about her horrific ordeal, *which I was*, and to give her pause for reflection before continuing. Truthfully, I had no idea whatsoever what to say or do, but I was also trying to be the man in this relationship, if you can catch-my-drift.

Time dragged by.

Time dragged by.

"May I ask what you liked to do when you were a child?" Ahh, the sweet perkiness of Cora's voice burst through the monotony of the scene yet again!

"As a child?" I chuckled.

"Yes!" she brightly reaffirmed.

"Well...I enjoyed fishing very much, still do."

"That's great," she beamed. "How often would you go? And where?"

"Pretty much any chance that I got. I'd head over to whatever nearby lake or river the locals were usin' and I'd pop my line in too."

"That's nice, did you catch much?"

"Always," I bragged. And it was true. "So," I announced, "what's something my darling Cora enjoyed as a precious youngster?"

"Boxing."

"What?!" Again she surprised me in the most delightful of ways. *How I loved this girl.*

"Yes, believe it or not Jonathan, I'd hop around demonstrating my best hooks and fancy footwork...all for show, of course. I've never hit anyone or anything!"

"Somehow I kinda figured that."

We laughed and it felt good once again to be good-humored and informal. Cora grinned with her usual beauty and I adored her cheeks as they blossomed in a rosy hue; her eyes wide with a rare clarity and sweet optimism that delightfully tickled my nerves.

"Aww, my little boxer Cora," I said.

Her unrelenting smile was all the reply that I needed.

5

Without hesitation, I met Cora the following afternoon for lunch at Carmen's Café. I suspected she wanted another one of Carmen's noted tarts, but she, of course, denied that jovially as soon as we walked through the door.

"Jonathan, we're here for lunch, not dessert!"

"Uh-huh," I teased. "Well I'm sure you'll make room for dessert later."

"I don't know," she quipped in return. "We'll see."

"Oh I'll be having dessert later so unless you want to sit there and just watch me devour it, you'll be having some too." Her giggles boosted me ego, as usual, and I expected the day to be fantastically thrilling.

"What can I get you folks?" the counter-server asked.

"I will be having a Cobb salad sandwich and a ginger ale," Cora announced.

"And for you sir?"

"Yes, I'll take a chicken soup with noodles, a Waldorf sandwich, and a lemonade."

"Sure, take a seat on the patio and I'll bring it on out to you folks."

I paid the server and offered a generous tip for our convenience. We headed towards the patio and Cora again selected the tiniest of tables.

"You like to sit in cramped spaces, dear?" I ragged.

"Ah, yes, Cora-sized!"

We parked ourselves and eagerly awaited our lunches, all the while gazing at each other with the kind of looks that would thaw even the iciest of hearts.

"Have you read the news this morning?" Cora inquired.

"No, I have yet to do that. Anything good?"

"Yes I found it quite remarkable that they're building another skyscraper in New York."

"Oh yes, the Empire State…that's begun, huh?"

"Indeed, it has."

Just then the young man from Carmen's brought forth our lunch and I immediately scooped a messy spoonful of chicken broth. I slurped it down and peered at Cora who, again, was slyly grinning in my direction.

"Sorry," I garbled.

"It's ok, sweetheart."

Was this the first time that she had referred to me in such a way? I think it was!

"I suppose I'm hungry," I stated obviously.

"It's alright. You go ahead and eat. I will too. We can talk afterward or I'll mutter us along, ha ha." Cora's pleasant nature could make any encounter comfortable, I surmised.

We munched away at our sandwiches and I offered Cora some soup. She declined but, I suspect, was preferential to my politeness. That was the goal, after all. The day was spectacular as the clouds were minimal and a cool breeze kept the sun from distracting our thoughts. A few birds harmonized beside us and a squirrel scurried through in hopes of obtaining a nibble of bread or a spare walnut. It reminded me of a cartoon skit aired prior to the main feature at the cinema. It was uncomplicated, candid, childlike.

Eventually, our cordial dialogue began.

"What is your definition of love, Jonathan?"

"Wow, Cora, you should be a journalist with your stunning questions!"

"Thanks."

"Well, let's see…I suppose to me love is the means of the true security we are all searching for. It's the cozy place to hang your hat, the bond that can give two people a home, a family, a shared faith. It's the joy of life, but also it's the challenge and probably more work than tending to the fields or studying each letter of the law."

"That's true."

"What would you say your definition is, beautiful?"

Gratifyingly embarrassed, Cora proceeded. "Now then, I would say that love is the greatest of all things, like 1 Corinthians says. It can heal every hurt; open every mind; and give purpose to even the seemingly-most meaningless of lives. It soothes and warms and is what we all seek to live for. It is my end-all, be-all; my one and only must-have dream; my idea of heaven on earth."

"Wow, that's a lot." My tone was blunt and my visage, I imagine, emotionless. I hadn't wanted to insult Cora but it was apparent that her idealistic vision of love was not only impractical but, perhaps, quite dangerous. People with such beliefs tended to be disappointed. You know, the higher you rise the harder you fall sort-of-thing.

"Oh."

Again, rescue the poor girl. "Don't take my response the wrong way, love. I am just a pragmatist because of the life I've lived. Your romanticism is inspiring to say the least. I would just hate to see you saddened or disappointed, that's all."

"Are you planning on disappointing me, Jonathan?" Now, her visage was grave.

"No."

"Good." That illuminated her, I could tell.

"I was just trying to point out that, for as magnificent as love is, it can also be unpredictable and tremendously taxing."

"You've been in love before?"

"Y--y--yes."

"Ah. Ok. Well you don't have to be nervous to tell me."

"No, I'm not."

"K. Well..."

"Should we talk about something else?"

"No. I think it's important to discuss this. Don't you, Jonathan?"

"Of course. It's key to share everything. Remember?" I hoped that by flashing her a charming smile it would alleviate the tension.

"Yes I remember. How many times would you say you've been in love?"

"Um," I took a long pause to think of what the answer really was, not to mention how to deliver it. "I'm not even sure Cora." I wiped the sweat from my brow and hunched over the table. The pressure was consuming me, although sensibly it was my own fault. I was the one pushing for constant openness, unwavering candor.

"How can you not be certain of something such as that?"

"I don't know."

"Now you care not to discuss it."

"No. I do. Please just give me a moment."

I arose from the table and walked to the edge of the patio, my back facing Cora to supply me a minute of lenience. I stared off at the birds who previously sang beautifully for us, never once glancing back at Cora to see her expression or if she was looking my way, too. The birds pecked at stale bread bits as though there could be something fresh and delicious underneath. Or maybe the fusty crumbs did satisfy them? In any case, their distraction functioned as a dreadfully needed gift in this jiffy, and I was indebted, to say the least.

"You are obliged to return to lunch," Cora bellowed my way.

"I am." I strolled back towards her, attempting to pull myself together as tidy as possible. It's amazing what a well-groomed look and a deep breath can do for a man in said situation. Upon reaching her chair I placed my right hand on her left shoulder and gently squeezed, just so she would know that my presence was straight. The confidence left within me was mustered forth and I sat in good posture and with every earnest attempt to avoid hypocrisy.

"Cora, I am a practice-what-you-preach kind of guy and since I said I require frankness from you, frankness is what you too will receive in return."

"Uncommon," she smiled. "Reciprocity is a delectable thing."

"Please just let me have the floor to speak for a few, love. I--I want to tell you everything, and as hard as that is to do, I can get through it all if you'll just listen…There have been loves in my life before. In different ways, if you follow me."

She shook her head no.

"Well, anyway," I continued, "I can appreciate that, but I'll do my best to explain as it is. The first time I thought I had fallen in love, well let's just say upon looking back, it was not love in any sense. The next occasion taught me that. That particular experience was falling into love, but it certainly wasn't the kind of true love I think we are both searching for and you are so proficient in describing. And this, too, was confirmed in the end…What I'm attempting, albeit poorly, to say Cora is that it takes a lot of awareness to recognize love and, upon finding it, even more commitment to carrying out the work and feeding the fires, you know?"

"Sure," she said, sounding completely dissatisfied with my response. "Although I'm not opposed to working hard," she added.

"Oh, I know that." Perhaps my reaffirmations would soothe her inquisition. "Well have we exhausted this topic?" I aspired with glee and the most hopeful of enthusiasms.

"No, not really," Cora edged in a tone of half comedic talent and half brazen sincerity. Even in her ever-present dainty splendor she could talk as the crow flies: directly straight and deadly uninterrupted. "But we shall revisit it at another hour!"

It was observable that she wanted to ease my anxiety which, by now, had even managed to scare the birds away.

"Ok, it's for another time," I conceded.

"Did you have something more to say, Jonathan?"

"No, love."

"Sure?"

"Yes, I'm sure."

"K. Well I--"

"I just want you to realize," I crudely interrupted, "that although love is not this birds-singing, sun-shining, life-is-perfect thing, it is...it is...it is--"

"all I need." Yes, we had voiced these three precious little words at the identical moment in time.

"It must be a sign," I articulated, unaware I was speaking out loud.

"I thought you didn't believe in signs," she coyly countered.

"Maybe I do and I didn't know it."

"Ohhh...see, the lessons do continue after the fact," she smarted.

"Yeah, that was *my* point earlier!"

"True," she avowed.

And it was true, after all.

6

$\mathcal{N}$early half my lifetime ago, as my adolescence winded down, there was a man I admired. No, he was not my father, nor his father, nor a pastor, an elder, or a family friend. He was a brawny, rugged, once-upon-a-time bartender from Baltimore. I know nothing of Baltimore and, I hate to admit, not much more of him than beyond flashes that stuck in my head. They're still branded there and, to this day, I keep on admiring the Bambino.

Maybe it was because Babe Ruth reminded me of the trains with which I had become so familiar. They too were bulky, dirty, powerful, and so good. Familiarity discomforts many, but not me. There are so few things that I've found familiar that they've all become tender to me in one way or another.

I keep thinking how talented Babe was in his youth and many recognized it at St. Mary's, so by the time he was years my junior now, he was already contracted to the Orioles. Minor league or not, he was on his way and that's more than I could say for myself. *Don't sound so pathetic.* What I mean is I have no freaking clue as to what I've done or what I *am* doing or what I *could be* doing. Other than for Cora, I have zilch. But Babe, man, he's done so much people don't even realize it. A cousin of a gent I rode the rails with saw the Sultan of Swat do a lot more than knock out those homers. Apparently the chap could pitch as fine as the best of 'em. I wish I had a sole skill that even half matched up to one of Babe's hidden talents.

Never let the fear of striking out get in your way, Babe once said. Now that was something I could understand. *Phew*, I'm using it in my relationship with Cora, there's no doubt. I just cannot give up on her because I believe in the love I'm feeling and what could become of us, in all our glory, is worth the fear I face. The way I figure, either we're gonna make it and be the finest couple to ever come out of the Dust Bowl, or we're going to crash and burn and that'll pretty much be the end of me. It's worth the risk.

So, speaking of fears, I dropped by a morning later to deliver Cora's over-blouse, which I had been hauling around since our luncheon at Carmen's. I suppose I was terrified of embarking upon another deep tête-à-tête and failing miserably at answering for myself. Naturally, worries consumed me as I deliberated that Cora may view me as unstable, like a train off its tracks—a weighty chunk of rusted iron, rickety and wobbly. Who wants that?

"Your lovely blouse," I stated handing over the garment, still impeccably pressed and smelling of her lilac perfume.

"Why thank you," she amorously replied. Her ripostes delighted me and I, in actual fact, woke up each morning with contemplation of her sweetness and quips permeating my psyche. "I'll just set this inside and be right out."

"Sure."

While I waited for Cora I mentally kicked around a few topics for discussion but, in the end, came up with nothing solid. Briefly I thought, *how would the Babe grapple with this situation?*, but I dismissed that swiftly once I comprehended that this was reality and, no, I was not the Babe. And then, she returned.

"So what's on the agenda for this afternoon?" she inquired.

"Uh, don't know." These words just stumbled out of my mouth.

"Ok...Any errands you need to knock out today?" *Knock out*, geez this gal was hilarious. Suddenly, I got the giggles.

"Jonathan?" First, she laughed playfully with me. Then there was the most uncomfortable aura, or so I believed based upon the reaction pasted to her face. Finally, she scolded me. "Jonathan, what's the matter with you!"

It took me several minutes to cease the silliness but, fortunately, I did. *Now, explain yourself, fool.*

"Excuse me for that, Cora. I apologize."

"Well I should hope so...I mean, no problem at all, but that was odd."

She didn't appear angry so I figured I was still in her good graces, but I needed an elucidation nonetheless.

"Look, there's no reason for me to be uncomfortable around you Cora, and I'm not—not at all—but sometimes I try so hard to please you and impress you and make myself appear worthy of you that I act just like a pure idiot. I am truly sorry, love. I am."

She's not saying anything. I presume she heard me? I guess I'll wait another few seconds for her to digest this apology.

I watched a bird fly overhead.

I kicked the dirt around with the tip of my worn shoe.

I glanced at Cora, then the sky, then Cora.

Still no word.

"Maybe I should elaborate, Cora."

"No. That's quite unnecessary."

"You were just making me sweat it out?"

"No," she chuckled. "There are a few thoughts on my mind but I too am learning in this relationship. I'm trying to be patient and that's a task for me to learn. We'll get there eventually, I'm sure."

I presumed she was serious and I took her at her word.

"Ok," I merely replied.

Obviously I have done a miserable job of unveiling my heart to Cora, but I also was determined to improve. I looked up again at the sky, now peeking back in between full, silvery clouds, and I wondered *how on earth could I save my foolish self?*

7

*L*ater that night Cora and I were to meet up for coffee, and I was buoyant by the opportunity to tell her of my surging feelings. As I sat in the dimly lit diner, swirling a cheap metal spoon on the table in a series of broad circles and awkward figure eights, a shadowy figure approached me. 'More coffee?' is what I expected to hear, but it was not so.

"Jonathan?"

"Yeah," I muttered, eerily looking up.

"It's me, Stephanie."

Standing poised before me was Stephanie Binfield, perfect posture, smooth skin, and brown eyes that sparkled even in the dark. She fluffed her already over-teased, over-curled hair and ran her palms down the front of her white cashmere sweater.

"Yes...hi." I was secretly hoping she would not recognize me but then my brain clarified on my behalf: *she already has.*

"May I?" She motioned towards the empty chair across from me, holding out her hand that was finely jeweled and tanned like buttered caramels.

"Sure," I hurried. Immediately I began glancing around the diner and flashing my eyes towards the front door. Rightly so, I was nervous of Cora spotting me sharing coffee with another young lady. *But maybe she isn't staying,* I conjured optimistically.

"Black coffee and a slice of lemon pie," she blurted to the waitress across the room.

It took all of my will to refrain from huffing or retorting for Stephanie to leave. She wasn't a rude or displeasing young woman, just unwanted in my current presence. I only could imagine myself with Cora now.

Stephanie continued the conversation and even managed to pause long enough to let me talk, too. But as the moments passed I became easy in her presence and time slid away like bubbly lava creeping along slippery black rocks. We nattered about poetry and cuisine, travel and foolish politics. I thought at one point that perhaps it would be best to keep that right eye of mine glued to the entrance door, but I did not. And, wouldn't you know, eventually Cora breezed in, spotted us mid-chat, and I had not detected it at all.

I can only piece together now, within my own mind of course, what it must have been that Cora witnessed. Excruciatingly I determined that she probably observed me flashing a fantastic grin to Stephanie and, for all I know, possibly read my lips or overheard a word or two of conversation. *Wait, what was it that I said?* I suppose I figured that whatever words passed between Stephanie and I, they were only words, after all, and unable to spoil our extraordinary relationship.

Upon escaping the diner I headed immediately to find Cora. I worried about my girl, how she must be feeling, and my mind raced hatefully. It took me two hours but then I spotted frail Cora sitting on a patio step outside of Carmen's, which had long since closed for the night. Her head drooped within her hands as though she was Atlas, attempting, albeit unsuccessfully so, to still hold up her world. She glanced at me as I approached and her eyes were dull and grey; her frown rigid.

"Can we talk?" was all I could think to ask.

"Sure."

"What did you see? Were you there tonight? What did you hear? Did you think you heard something?" I couldn't stop.

She austerely shook her head no and, simultaneously, the tears free-flowed all the way down to her chin, her knees, and the dirty street.

"Then what's wrong—what's the matter?" My heart raced, fluttered, quivered, all the way to panic attack speed now.

"I don't know."

"Just calm down. Breathe! Think. Tell me what you need. I'm here."

"I don't know."

"Cora I'm interested in you; deeply, truly interested."

"I know."

"And I mean this sincerely. I can't imagine myself with another woman now. I've been down that path before--"

"Oh--"

"I mean I've been down the path of choosing the wrong woman and what I've learned is you gotta pick the right one from the start!"

"Yes!" she hatefully agreed.

"I realize you know this because you're so smart and self-assured and all that, but, me, I have to learn things the hard way sometimes. Wouldn't you know it?"

"Yes."

"And, like I've been sayin', what I've learned is I can't twist another girl into the right woman. All that crap about molding a girl into the woman she needs to become is just that: crap. It's a bunch of malarkey, Cora! I say, pick the right one from the beginning… and you…Cora, you're the right one."

I flung my arms down to my sides and gasped in a huge breath. My lungs full of air, I still felt like I was suffocating, but I stood in reverence of her impending response.

"Cora, please." Exhausted as I was, I wasn't above begging.

"Ok," she wiped the smeared charcoal from her eyes and neatened her soiled clothes. I'd never witnessed Cora as such a crushing mess before. It stimulated my guilt, to say the least. "Well then let's sit down." She motioned to the edge of the curb and we sat; the crumbled concrete a fine spot for me but not for a woman as exquisite as Cora.

"We should sit at a table," I stood up and insisted.

"No." She grabbed my elbow and tugged me back down. I obliged. "I want to know everything—about each woman. Leave nothing out...if I know about it, I can deal with it. I'm not good with surprises Jonathan."

"Alright." *Jeez, how was I going to go through with this?* I paused, reflected, then spoke. "I have had loves before, Cora. Or at least I thought they were loves at the time. In hindsight, I was wrong, and I can admit I'm wrong when I am--," I stared at her head-on so she would get my point, "but I learned my lesson the hard way."

"Yeah, you said that already."

"I'm trying to talk here!"

"Well talk in specifics, Jonathan!"

"Alright!!" I was losing my cool. Quickly I apologized and waited a moment for each of us to be composed. I continued and decided to start with the worst. "I was in a pretty serious relationship once. Yes, I had other relationships, too, but this...this, was quite serious. It was important to me, at that particular time, and it was sobering when it was over with. I never thought I'd meet someone again who interested me so much...that was, until you."

Cora's eyes were glazed over and she was half-staring at the ground and half in a trance. I knew she was processing every word I was saying and it must have been hurting her already. Desperately I longed to reach out to her and hold her close to my chest, but now wasn't the time. There was only time for candor.

"Who was she?" Cora asked.

"Her name was Cheryl. I met her in Texas and we had a deep year together. We grew close rather early on and things moved pretty rapidly. A lot happened during that time. We got engaged and--"

"You were engaged?!"

Sigh.

"Yes, I was. I--"

"You mean you proposed to a girl and everything?!!!"

"Cora. Yes. Would you let me explain? Please, allow me that much."

"Ok," she puffed out and swallowed, attempting still to screen her tears. "Sorry."

"It's alright. Look I know this is uncomfortable for you…"

"Uncomfortable!"

"Painful then, what-have-you…It's hard for me too, don't you think?"

"Yes, I'm sure that it is. It just hurts so much to hear all this, Jonathan." Now she was sobbing uncontrollably. Through her tears she let out, "It kills me to know this because I'm truly in love with you."

"I know, baby. Come here." I pulled her weak spirit into my body and wrapped my arms securely around her. If I could soothe her, everything would be fine. I had to believe that because I couldn't lose my Cora. I repeatedly whispered 'I'm sorry,' 'you're my girl,' and 'I adore you, only you' into her ears. I kissed her forehead, brushed her hair with my fingertips, and rocked her gently on my lap. I had never felt so close to another human being before. Not even during the moments of intimacy which I had yet to speak of to Cora.

"Please, continue," she at long last garbled.

I repositioned her into a seated position and encouraged her to be strong and composed. This would all be over soon and nothing ever would come between us again.

"Cora, you must know. I know part of you doesn't want the full story now, but the sooner I tell you the sooner it can be part of the past and then we will know all of each other's souls through and through. That's what we need...You still want that, right?"

She nodded decisively. "Yes."

"I lost my virginity to Cheryl."

I expected to hear her scream 'what,' shout to the Lord, burst into a waterfall of tears, *something*. She was stone silent.

Minutes later she asked, "How did it happen?" She had wanted to know if it was planned or in the moment. I promised to oblige and answer all her questions. I told her it happened unexpectedly after we had become engaged. We were in a grassy field, on the most beautiful of cool, summer days, alone, and it was that old one-thing-led-to-another bit. I kept my tone serious because I didn't want her to conclude that it wasn't a significant moment. It was. And that was what bothered me about it. I lost something...well, worse, gave away something, that I'd never get back. Truly that *something* belonged to Cora. Yes, Cora who had her gift ripped away from her, against her will.

"I don't know if I can ask this but if I don't I'll keep wondering."

"Then, just ask," I encouraged.

"Did...did...ugh!"

"It's ok. Really. You should ask. We're talking; we're being open. This is what it's all about." *Yeah, the torturing of Jonathan.*

"Did you enjoy it?"

I thought for a while. Not that it was a trick question. I'm sure both her curiosity and her jealousy prompted the question. Frankly, I would have wondered the same if our roles were reversed.

"No," I stated. "Honestly I thought it was going to be special. So much more than a physical act, you know? But truly at the time I didn't even enjoy the physical, uh, relief of it. And emotionally, the intimacy just wasn't there. Sure, there were times the devastation of that whole thing not working out crushed me. Mostly because she left and then I felt abandoned and, well, I guess I got a bit of an abandonment complex. But she didn't satisfy me in any way that a woman should. I guess I was desperate, I'm sorry."

"Desperate for what?"

"I'm terrified of having no one, ok! Because I never have." My frustration was evident and I speedily wiped my sweaty forehead and apologized for raising my voice.

"It's fine, really," she calmly avowed.

Just then I began to sob, which I never do. Especially in front of someone, like a woman. But I couldn't help myself; my emotions were uncovered and out of control. I, too, am only human and it grieved me to be damaged goods. *Men shouldn't think such notions… Yeah, but I do.*

Upon salvaging my equanimity I addressed Cora for a few more remarks.

"Do you wish to know about the others? The less-significant relationships?"

"No, suppose not."

"Are you sure?"

"Yes."

"You can ask again later, if you like."

"Ok…thank you."

"Sure."

We lingered.

I said, "I'm sorry for I know how much this must devastate you…to hear of the engagement and the sexual relationship."

"It does." The tears emanated from her now-troubled eyes and flowed along her cheeks and neck like a river whose current meanders chaotically. She insisted once more that everything was 'alive and well' between us, but that she needed to depart for the rest of the day. I acquiesced, without a choice, and provided my apologies and earnest love as best as I could. Too numb to draw upon any better words, we left, both of us tattered and wounded.

8

$\mathcal{I}$ didn't quite know what I had done, but I knew it wasn't good. *Was it a crime to break a young woman's heart?* It may as well be.

I tried reaching Cora throughout the next day, and evening, and morning-noon-night thereafter. But no such luck. Wondering if there was one thing worth saying anyway, I shuffled around town, kicking stones with my worn steel-toed boots and tossing splintered toothpicks to the wind after I had nervously chomped them unrecognizable.

Perhaps Cora couldn't always muster up such empathy; *she* was only human after all. How difficult it must be to fall in love with a man of my nature, of my past. There was little of worldly substance I could offer her and even less that I could say to erase the torrid thoughts I presumed she pieced together after our most recent conversation. I could not imagine a man's hands upon Cora and yet I had committed such wrongdoings, and more, with another woman.

I began to conclude that it was reasonably in Cora's best interests that I cease to contact her. She didn't need this, me, whatever, in her potential-filled life. And, yet, as the minutes ticked past my mind recalled Cora's innocent eyes, consumed with love and necessity for me, and the selfishness of having pondered the abandonment of this lovely creature gnawed at my pathetic conscience. How will I leave her be? *I can't do it.*

Most of those evenings were wasted, muttering about the city like the hobo that I am; thinking, considering, yet concluding nothing. And then I surmised the worst plan of all. I, too, was petrified of enduring alone. My whole life was spent wrangling, scraping, gouging through the earth. I've had no home, no family, and no opportunities. It's long been just Jonathan and this country, struggling through years of poverty and depression. America and I, two dry wastelands with few solid schemes for recovery and repair. But I, *yes I*, now had one.

My plan, as appalling as it may now sound, involved little more than the attempt to pursue two females: Stephanie and Cora. It read objectionable, as it should, but I justified it with the perception that either young lady could easily locate another suitor should things manage to not work themselves out. Needless to mention, I went with it and that was that.

This same evening I arranged to cross paths with Stephanie. I had encountered a mutual acquaintance during my city wanderings and been informed that she would attend a school booster in Wellsville around suppertime. Her father's construction company frequently bid upon governmental and commercial proposals and, with the economy in a constant downward spiral, one was expected to attend school events, church gatherings, fairs and all, for even a shot at a project. I think the nosedive of the depression worsened her parents' spirits so Stephanie jangled through soirées and fanfares on their behalf. It was certainly admirable, I persuaded myself to believe.

Doting my cleanest trousers and one-and-only white button up shirt, I arrived at the Wellsville gymnasium, derby in one hand and the other smoothing aside my poor combing job. Right away, I spotted Stephanie. *Avoid idle chit-chat and approach the woman; take her.*

"No, I'll play it level this time," I mouthed to my ego.

I slid through the crowd of families and poor businessmen; yet all of them gleefully sporting broad smiles and chuckling delightfully. The building was bright, sweetly decorated with spirit streamers, and bursting with smells of buttered popcorn and cinnamon apple tarts.

'Hello there' and 'howdy' passersby pecked my way. I was too attentive to retort, like a blackbird stamping over the grubby ground, head bopping to-and-fro, seeking nothing but its beak's content.

"Such a pleasure to see you," I said to Stephanie, my words sleek and my demeanor handsomely mellow.

"And to you," she smiled and then paused. "Stephanie Binfield," she reached her hand out like a queen awaiting her servant's kiss. But then she grinned and giggled, it was all in good humor. "What brings you here this evening, sir?" she teased, but I would not fall prey tonight.

"You." *Yeah, show her how serious you can be.*

"Oh," she blushed. "I'm flattered. And might I say you look incredibly fine this evening?"

"You might...but will you?" I was cooler than any silver screen desperado: masculine, confident, achingly arrogant.

"Yes." Then she spoke nothing more.

We walked through the gathering and at times purposefully brushed each other's arm or hand. Just as the master of ceremonies sought the crowd's attention my palm inched around Stephanie's left hand, caressing every fragment from the ring on her mid-finger to the crevices around her knuckles to the smooth texture of her manicured nails. She responded so delicately that I was uncertain of the pleasure it brought her.

"That is truly nice," she breathed finally.

I glowed in response and pleaded with my heart to cease pains for Cora. Throughout that evening Stephanie and I danced and strolled, drank punch, munched caramel popcorn, and even consumed a couple glasses of sparkling wine, courtesy of her father. I realized my plan was not only plausible but perfection. My heart, my soul longed for Cora, but if I could not have her nor manage her emotions then Stephanie would delight me, my body, and provide prospects that presently evaded me.

This is wrong. But I did it anyway.

9

After the booster social Stephanie and I left together. How we moved from acquaintances to a full-fledged couple in a mere four hours was beyond me, but a relationship of sorts was progressing and it served no interest to halt it.

"Can I persuade you out for coffee?" she asked.

I paused, wrestling still with my own damn conscience. "Of course, C--." Oh Lord in heaven I nearly misspoke. *What to say now?* I paused, my mind blank. *What the fuck do I say?* Still no sign of a pending reaction from Stephanie. "Um…did you hear me?"

"Huh?" she giggled. "Um, sure!"

Good thing Stephanie isn't that sharp of a listener. Dear Cora always hung on to each of my words. Suddenly then I wished for the divine ability to undo time and erase the evening.

"Did you have a good time tonight?" Stephanie spoke, right on cue.

"Of course," I voiced with forced optimism.

"Say something other than 'of course,' silly!"

Nervously I laughed. It was all I could bear to do. Really I've never been cut out for the playboy lifestyle.

"We'll stop at Carmen's and see if they're still open for drinks. I bet she still has a pot on." Wow, who knew Stephanie was such a know-it-all?

Nevertheless, I nodded in agreement and focused solely on driving.

"You look tense."

"No," I choked. "I just don't want to damage your father's car, of course." Ugh, there I go again.

"Well…maybe this will help." Stephanie leaned in close to my right side and simultaneously put her lips on my neck and her hand on my crotch. She gripped me firmly and my hands jerked the wheel, barely sustaining control. Rather than losing her composure and expressing any ounce of feminine frailty, as every other female alive would have, Stephanie snickered boisterously, like I had committed the driving infraction intentionally for her entertainment.

"Maybe I oughtta pull over," my poor grammar began to leak through as did my trademark unconfident personality.

"Yeah, park somewhere," she teased, half her body atop me now, her exposed thigh hovering over my own. I glanced momentarily at Stephanie, the curves of her cleavage on full display, a glimpse of her white panties glowing in the darkened car.

"So here we are," I motioned for her to be properly seated.

"We're not at Carmen's yet, Jonathan," she said, still laughing away.

"Oh, right. But we're close."

"No we're not." Her coy voice stroked my still-throbbing flesh. I raced like a madman to the café and prayed earnestly that we would be delayed by chatter amongst friends or acquaintances. No such luck. As we arrived there was only one light on inside and the open sign was hastily whisked away. "Oh are they not open?" Stephanie shyly inquired.

"Let's see! They must be!" I darted out of the car and made a beeline towards the door. "Still open for coffee!!" I commanded, not questioned. The gentleman inside appeared gruelingly exhausted but granted my demand nonetheless. I whipped my head back and mouthed to Stephanie to come in.

"Get 'em to go," she spat.

Making no attempts to disguise it I rolled my eyes and with embarrassment requested two take away coffees with heavy cream.

"I'll make 'em fresh," the gentleman added.

A mere twelve minutes later I exchanged pocket change for those two coffees and fretted back to the car. Stephanie sat poised inside, finger-teasing her coif and smearing a Vaseline-looking substance onto her lips. I passed the cups through her passenger window and rather than thanking me for the late night refreshment she uttered, "Hurry up an' get in!" Her smile was an aphrodisiac; that was undisputable.

I paced my way to the driver's door and slowly grasped the handle to pop it open. I plopped inside and quickly swayed myself to act normal, pleased, self-assured.

"What...would you...like to do...now?" Stephanie slipped the words through her mouth in slow motion and, I admit, it made me ache. *Damn, she's got powers over me already, too?*

"Uh, go for a ride and drink our coffees?"

"Well, but should we really drink and drive? We wouldn't want to spill the coffee in Daddy's car and you know what a klutz I am!"

"Ok. So what would you suggest?"

"Let's just park and drink them...and talk."

I couldn't bear to keep debating with the girl so I grudgingly acquiesced.

"Is this fine?" I sought her approval as I pulled into an empty lot about half a mile away.

"Sure!"

Before the motor cooled Stephanie already slithered close to me again and snuck her left arm behind my neck. Eerily I glanced over and peering back at me were her sparkling eyes, creamy white smile, and damp, rosy lips. How could I not succumb to this feminine lure? Any man would, attached or otherwise.

"You know, I genuinely do like you," she said with definitive sincerity.

"Thanks."

"You like me too...or not in that way?"

"Which way would that be?"

"You know!"

"Ah," I laughed. I couldn't resist, her bashfulness was amusingly cute. "Sure I like you the same way." *That's right, stick with the plan, brother.*

"Well then…" She slanted towards the dash and paused just long enough for me to make a move. I could tell that was her intention; it would be obvious to any gent. "Don't you wish to kiss me?"

"I don't want our coffees to get cold." *You're chicken, you dunce!*

"Who cares about the coffee?" Again, half-giggly, half-sultry. I couldn't stand firm. My blood rushing got the bigger of me.

I gripped her whole body and jammed hers against mine, my lips forcefully against hers, my hands pinning her arm and her wrist as I squeezed her ribcage and began ripping off her blouse. We kissed, first dry lips, then wet lips, then full tongue. It was the most aggressive make out session conceivable. In less than five minutes time I not only had half her shirt removed, but also her hair tensely pulled by my grip, her bra impelled aside from her left breast, my lips suctioned to the bare nipple, and one finger under her skirt to ferret for wet panties. They were wet and my testosterone urged me further. I began violently rubbing her through her panties, all the while kissing her as hard, and she moaned from both the ecstasy and, I'm sure, the pain of my touch. Her hips rocked back and forth while she sat face-to-face on my lap, only pausing from frenching me to moan and stare into my eyes to convey the pleasure I was giving her. Her cries grew louder, and she rocked remorselessly, and then out-of-nowhere, she forced her panties to the side and slid my finger into her. I'd never seen or felt a woman's orgasm, but I presume that's what this was by the shaking of her thighs, the tousling of her hair, and the succulence on my hand. Her satisfaction entranced me; I'd tackle the throbbing of my body later on my own.

"Was it good?" I thought to ask senselessly.

"Yesss…"

Wow.

"Do you want me to rub it?" she cooed.

"Um, no thanks. I mean, I'm sure that would be great. But, no thanks. Rain check," I nervously muddled.

"K!" Stephanie was all smiles now. *So, there is power in a female orgasm.* Amidst my thoughts she said, "This doesn't make you think differently of me, does it?"

"Of course not, silly." And really it didn't. She was fast, that was undisputable. But as long as a girl didn't get around I was into her liking gratification. Plus, Stephanie had an innumerable amount of fantastic traits: social, humorous, pretty, and generous. A first-rate catch, she was. Yet, the exhilaration didn't stop the guilt. Somewhere my Cora was alone, perhaps saddened, or worse still, with another. *How could I have done such a thing?* Cora would never do this.

As quickly as she erupted, I took Stephanie home. My plan was undoubtedly successful, but only half of the waters had been tested. Now, to find Cora, and seal the deal.

The following morning I raced looking for Cora and upon locating her I jostled myself into the right frame of mind.

"Hey you!" I cheered her way.

"Hello. I'll walk over," she submitted.

"How are ya kiddo?"

"Just fine, thank you. What's going on with you, Jonathan? You seem funny."

"What?! Me?! No, silly! Aww, you're such a cutie when you worry."

"Huh?"

"Nothin'. Come on! Let's go have a blast today."

She laughed in a fit of hysterics. It offended me slightly, but acutely bruised my about-to-burst ego.

"Well, it's a new you, huh?" She smarted to me.

"Sure. What's wrong with that?"

"Nothin', silly," Cora mocked.

"It's not funny." Just then I let my face show all of my guilt and worries from the prior night because Cora blurted 'what have you done' in the worst tone audible. *Say you haven't done anything, idiot!*

Birds chirp, leaves rustle in the breeze, a girl rings her bike bell as she darts by.

I said zilch.

"Oh, ok. Well you don't have to tell me, it's fine," she maintained. Her composure was incredible. I never would have accepted a woman's silence as an answer. "What happened to the man I first met, Jonathan?"

"Whattya mean? I'm right here."

"No you're not."

"I don't know what you're talking about. *You* don't know what you're talking about." Again I scoffed my toe about the grass and dirt, staring downward to avoid her beaming eye-contact.

"I do. But it's fine, you don't have to tell me, like I said."

"No?"

"Nope. Lucky for you," she walked away gabbing as though part of a soliloquy, "I'm already in love. I can't help but accept you and whatever you bring into this relationship. I wish for only goodness from and for both of us; but those are just my silly-girl requests. I'll take what may come my way."

"You possess so many beautiful qualities, Cora." Lord knows I don't deserve this girl.

"The only real possession you'll ever have is your own character."

I nodded.

"Thomas Wolfe. My favorite author."

"Ah."

"Jonathan, listen to me." Cora nimbly picked up my hand and rested her palm against my own. She parlayed some more but I thought of nil besides causally exploring Stephanie's body and how overwhelmingly wrong it was. "...Whatever you're torturing yourself regarding, don't." Those were Cora's final words that day and how could I not embrace her compassion and wisdom? I broke down again before her and realized I could hide nothing. She knew there was a transgression of some sort, though I doubt she suspected this calamity. But, alas, she moved her lips as though there was something supplementary to say.

"Love won't let me turn back."

Then, nothing more.

10

Lessons are not wasted on me. I erred once against Cora, one time undoubtedly too many, but I was refreshed with a determination to be the right man in her life. Later that week, I penned a letter to Stephanie.

> *Dear Stephanie,*
> *You truly are a darling girl and you know I think quite highly of you. My, your sense of humor and charming social quips are something else! I admire you, with all sincerity. I have to say you provided me one of the most memorable nights of recent times and I applaud your boldness and buoyancy. You pepped me up and you're a doll for doing that! Thanks, dear!*
> *Well, I surely hate to say it but I think we had better cool down for a bit, ya know? I figure I need some time to work on myself, being the oddball boy I am. Ha ha. Anyway then, take care and I'll be chatting with you soon, no doubt.*
> *Smile for me,*
> *Jonathan*

There. I did it. It was high time I focused solely on Cora before I lost her to a smarter gent. As soon as I mailed the letter to Stephanie I headed directly to Cora's. Along the way I paused at Brown's

Book-Shop and jotted down a few words she may appreciate. When I arrived, rather than attempting to speak with eloquence and acumen, I slid the slip of paper into her little hand. She fumbled with it momentarily, then opened it and read aloud: *"A young man is so strong, so mad, so certain, and so lost. He has everything and he is able to use nothing...Hmm..."*

"Yes, more Thomas Wolfe."

"Oh, really? I wasn't familiar with this quote."

"Oh."

"But it's a good one!" she reassured.

I smiled, proud of myself for displaying some sense of academia and forethought. My ego was healthily reestablished, that is, until Cora questioned me on the passage.

"What made you select this quote to give me? How did it speak to you, would you say?"

Cripes, woman, I don't know it's just a quote.

"Well," I spoke with calmness; pausing and displaying a thinking pose immediately thereafter, "it's really interesting. You know, it's pretty good in the way of speaking what's on my mind. Um...well, it's, it's--"

"It's ok, nevermind!" she laughed it off rather sweetly.

Needless to say, this drove me crazy. There are a lot of things I can tolerate, but being made a fool of in front of my lady was not one of them. I had to prove myself to her; this is something only a man thinking of marriage can understand. What is feels like, oh Lord, to show that woman you're not only good enough, but you're the best man she will encounter. I want to be her all; I need her to admire me. This isn't my ego gabbing, this is my manhood on trial here.

"No. It's fine, I have an answer," I demanded.

She paused, an enormously confused look on her mild-mannered face. "Ok?"

I cleared my throat deafeningly.

"Cora, I picked this quote for you because even though I realize I have little to offer you, in terms of tangibles and all, I do have some talents and skills and, hopefully, something that's attractive!" We laughed pleasantly together. "And so then," I slid my hand through my hair and inhaled heartily, "I don't feel like I have everything, like Wolfe mentioned, but I have my fair share and, even though I'm ready to offer it all to you, I don't know what to do with it because—because I'm lost, ok. I'm lost because I am not good alone--"

"Most men aren't." She was half serious, half giggly.

"True. I just think you should realize that even a man in the prime of his confidence and sense of self is insecure. Basically…we're all made secure through the love of that one woman."

"That's beautiful," she wept.

"Thanks." I clutched her hand and it felt better than ever. It soothed my insecurities, ignited my future, and excited that male ego of mine. She was my revelation.

We moseyed through the grass nearby and enjoyed the peace of the sun, the breeze, and the comfort of each other.

"So do you have plans for next weekend?" I blurted.

"No," she hysterically laughed.

"Ok, ok. You don't haveta double over," I coolly replied.

"I am most definitely available, sir!"

"Yeah?"

"Yeah," she whispered, staring tigerishly into my eyes. I was fixated on hers as well and I took that moment for what it was truly worth. I held her face delicately, charily pulled it towards me, and embraced her lips against my own. Her taste was sweet like ripe summer raspberries and soft, tender, moist, like maraschino cherries poised atop the creamiest sundae.

"Do you wish to accompany me to a new city?"

"Ooh, something new," she teased. "Sure, why not!"

And, just like that, my problems were again subsided.

11

That weekend Cora and I traveled to Coffeyville, a small Kansas town about a hair from the Oklahoma border. I had long thought about heading in that direction because soon after the city's discovery of natural resources, including gas sold cheaply to local builders, jobs appeared at glass factories and jar canning companies. A thousand people were working at the fruit jar factory alone, if you can believe it.

We strolled through the main strip of town and noted all of the little shops and fine brick plants. Coffeyville was also blessed with large deposits of limestone, shale, and some granite. Half a million bricks were created on slow days, then shipped near and far. Known as Coffeyville bricks, they were stamped with all sorts of sayings and designs, from basket weaves to floral patterns to architecturally-sound geometric shapes to "Don't Spit on Sidewalk."

"Do you like them?" I asked Cora.

"What? The bricks?"

"Yeah."

"Sure." She sounded only semi-enthused but I took advantage of having her undivided attention.

"Would you like one?"

"What?" She realized I was talking about an unsightly, grubby brick and began to laugh uncontrollably. "You're not serious?"

153

I stood frozen, staring at Cora's eyes, not so much as a blink or a flinch.

"Jonathan?"

About a block earlier I had detected a crow bar perched beside the Mason factory, adjacent to the gravel alley. Without deliberating for another moment, without uttering one word to Cora who looked overwhelmingly confused, I dashed towards Mason's to snatch the crow bar. Like a well-trained sprinter I beamed en route to my target and obtained it with ease. Huffing and panting perceptibly I, in no way, slowed my pace on the way back. Had I paused and saturated my brain with Cora's visage I may have ceased my adventure, but it was not so. With no trouble I stabbed the end of the crow bar in between two random sidewalk bricks and wrathfully hoisted the bar up and down to rip up one of the planted bricks.

"Jonathan, stop!" Cora urged as I neared the completion of my scheme.

The brick popped up, dirty and wet underneath, a hidden worm emerging as well. I gripped my accolade and admired it assiduously. The clay-colored, solid, hole-permeated, man-made rock, in all its masculine beauty and practical utility, was a work of art and, too, the simple man's need. Enough mental dissection, time for revealing my purpose.

"Here," I plunked the filthy brick into Cora's immaculate hands.

"Uh, what?!" she snipped.

"It's for you," I simply stated.

"Oh. Why, thank you," she strained.

Cora cautiously evaluated the brick as though it was the murder weapon from a horrific crime or a newborn baby that, if dropped, would necessitate a coroner, too.

"It's admittedly not the most romantic gift," I began.

"No. I love it! I appreciate the offer so much!" she appeased.

"Do you really?"

"Yes, of course, Johnny boy!"

She persisted in tumbling the stone again and again in her hands as though with each toss something new, and more beautiful, would be revealed.

"It's just a brick all around," I said disappointedly.

"Jonathan, I love it. Truly. It stands for something. *You* stand for something. So for you to present me with such a piece is like bequeathing me a piece of you. I couldn't love anything more." *She meant it.*

There was something else that needed to be said, whether it was the time or not.

"Cora, do you think we are both ready for this?"

"By 'this' I presume you mean us?"

"Yes."

"Well," she paused for a long time; she appeared both perplexed and annoyed by the question. Perhaps I shouldn't have said it. Her lack of lexis continued and I was dumbfounded. Desperately I wanted to go back and eat my foolish words. "I don't know," she finally announced. "I guess I can't answer for both of us."

"Uh-huh." I'm certain my embarrassment was written all over my clumsy face.

"I'll just answer for myself," cheerfully she proclaimed. "I'm ready!" Her joy, like the sun, pierced through me with comfort and passion, starting at my reddened face all the way down to my inner gut. Cora controlled my ego and my soul and I wished I could tell her that. "Are you ready?"

Pulling myself together I responded, "I am boldly ready."

She laughed in another fit of cute hysterics. It wasn't a shot at me, I easily concluded, but, rather, the bridge to moving on to a better point of conversation.

"It was a worthless question, I know."

"It's fine, Jonathan. There was a reason, subconscious or not, that you needed to ask. You did. It's done. And we're going to be okay."

"Yes we are. So do you like your brick?"

"I completely adore it." *And she w-a-s serious.*

"Well, I know it's not a diamond bracelet or earrings or whatever nice things girls expect and you deserve, but it's--"

"It's a sign of your creativity!"

I chuckled jollily. "Yes, that I suppose is true. But it's also something I guarantee I've never given before or will again *and* I doubt you'll run across another lady with such a lovely treasure."

"Agreed."

We prolonged our stay along Main Street, noting all of the delightful candy and treasure shops, and chatting up intensely the merits of the warehouses and factories too. Pausing momentarily in front of Ball Brothers' Glass Factory, Cora pressed her curious visage against the dirty, cracked side window to view the inner workings. She seemed inspired and awe-struck, although I doubt she was familiar with any of the machinery or operations.

Just then, "I want to go inside!" she delighted.

"I think they're closed, sweetheart."

"No, I want to go inside," she demanded again, negating my reply.

"Darling, they are not open. And even if they were I doubt they would allow us to stroll through, being they're cautious about safety and all--"

"Let's be bad…let's sneak in!" she giggled. *She really can't pull off this bad-girl persona very well.*

"Gee, Cora, I don't know."

"Come on! Pleeeeease!" Her innocent eyes staring up at me, her little girl hands posed together as though she was praying, her entire frame humbly and submissively before me, I caved.

"Alright. But stay behind me! I need you to be careful."

"But of course," inoffensively she replied.

We circled around three quarters of the building before I caught a glimpse of a propped window. Presumably it was left open for ventilation and not trespassing, but it was the most harmless means of entry.

"Here." I pointed to a spot on the ground, alerting Cora of my wishes for her to remain in one spot and let me figure out the felony. I crept to the window as though someone may hear me, pause, and shoot.

"There's no one around, silly."

I turned around, nearly annoyed. "I realize that. Now stay put, and wait for my word."

"K."

Frankly, it was all too easy to push the flimsy window fully open, hop aboard the window pane, and slide my way through. Not a scratch on me, *howdoya like that?*

"I'm in," I shouted back to Cora, as though she hadn't watched my presence escape hers.

"K, open the door, open the door!"

I unlatched the rusty bar lock across the side door and flung it open for Cora's entrance.

"My lady," I said, motioning with my hand for her unveiling.

"Why thank you," she kindly retorted, extending her hand in the most feminine of fashions. I kissed it, guided her in, and slammed the heavy door behind us.

Cora and I meandered around together, taking in the sights as though visiting a historic museum, complete with velvet ropes, guards, and all. We touched nothing, discussed little, and respected the scene scrupulously. The best American workers labored here, and we dared not to insert ourselves into their noble profession.

"Ooooowwwww!!!!" Cora let out the most piercing, bloodied

scream and I could not comprehend what had happened; I hadn't let my eyes off of her but for two seconds.

"What! What! Fuck, Cora, what is it!" I shrieked, darting towards her even though she was merely two feet away.

She revealed her hands and they were covered in tiny pools of burgundy blood. Droplets descended onto her tidy clothes, her shaking hands unable to control the messy viscousness.

"Hold on Cora, stay still." She was going into rapid shock and I fretted my own reaction and impotency to respond. I flung my shirt off and wrapped it frantically around both hands. She squealed in pain, presumably from both my aggression and the wounds themselves. 'It's ok baby' was all I could think to say. And I repeated it endlessly until we arrived back at the side door.

"But wait! My brick!"

She had composed herself simply long enough to vocalize four words.

"I'll get it, stay here, stay still!" I darted murderously fast towards where Cora had been standing and snatched the brick off a table. I precluded in that moment that Cora must have accidentally grabbed a piece of the nearby, ice pick-sharp broken glass, but who knew? It did not matter; and I did not pause long enough to determine the cause. I returned to her, realizing her shivering, pale state was anything but good. I was scared out-of-my-living-fucking-mind.

Circumspectly, I guided Cora outside and worried not one bit about the posterior door. *We should have never trespassed to begin with.* Frantic and confused, I spotted a couple walking down the street and shouted to them for help. They dashed towards us, in obvious horror of Cora's state.

"What is it, young man?" the man said.

"My girlfriend, Cora, this is her," I gabbed and gasped concurrently, "please help, she's been cut on her hands, we were in the glass factory, we should not have been, please help, she's lost blood and is weak, *please--*" Tears drizzled from my eyes; my dearest Cora, again I had not protected her.

"Ok, alright," the mother inserted, taking Cora's hands into her own and evaluating them calmly but swiftly. "She'll need stitches or at least suitable wrappings. Come. We'll take you."

We traveled with the couple, the Smiths, and Cora's wounds were properly cared for, by someone other than me, of course. I was in a trance. I disappointed her, myself too, and was cold, inconsolable, hushed as the plethora of cuts was cleaned, cleaned again, and wrapped repeatedly. By the end of it all we were exhausted and Cora's hands were tiny no more. She looked as though she was sporting three pairs of mittens, and I looked like a failure of a man, I surmised.

"Take me home," she whimpered.

"Of course," I agreed.

We thanked the Smiths repeatedly and they encouraged us to stay in touch. They were good folks, the best the area could have to offer, and it was by the grace of God that we encountered them.

"They were nice," Cora uttered as we left the hospital.

"Yes."

We said nothing else along the way home. She appeared dog-tired and disheveled—a look I had yet to see previously on Cora. But she was resplendent and remarkable nonetheless. I prayed silently that she would not blame me for this and in the coming days our relationship would heal along side of her hands.

"What is it?" she finally asked.

"Nothin'. Just worried about you. Feeling bad…and sorry, for letting this happen."

"It wasn't your fault." She slumped back in the seat, only a blank gaze on her drained face now.

"Relax, honey. We can talk later."

"Don't be upset, Jonathan," she maintained. "I should have listened to you. It was my idea to go in."

She began to cry frenziedly and it upset me even more. My feelings were completely out of control; I was ragged, but high, off of adrenaline and emotion.

"Don't cry, I beg of you, sweetheart!"

"Do you think it was a sign?" she questioned through her frequent sobs.

"A sign?! A sign of what?!" I shouted with raw sentiment and blood-pumping testosterone.

"I don't know," she bawled. "A sign of bad things to come for us?" I could barely understand her amidst her sniffles and yelps.

"Of course not, Cora." I pulled over long enough to cradle her until her tears desiccated and she was nearly asleep in my arms. I finger-combed her hair and kissed her sweaty forehead. "Everything will be ok, Cora. You taught me that."

She smiled, soothed and reassured, and I took her home to rest.

12

It was inevitable, but a few days passed before we met up again. The feeling was odd, admittedly so, because Cora and I were accustomed to spending a lot of time together. It bothered me a little, overall, because I realized Cora needed to unwind due to the nightmare at the glass factory. Clearly it wasn't as though she was having an enjoyable holiday. When I finally saw her I avowed to myself that I would ensure a peaceful, safe afternoon.

"My girl, so good to see ya! You are a vision of loveliness, that's for sure!" I intensely sought to emit exuberance and joy alone.

"Hi, Johnny boy, good to see you too!...You don't mind me calling you that, do you?"

"You can call me whatever you like as long as you call me yours."

"Awww..." *She's impressed, this is working.* "What plans do you have for us today, a safety class?"

Laughter. "We're heading to the train tracks, just to hang out. I'm up for a day of sitting in the sun, with my best girl, doing little more than shallow thinking or chatting away."

"Sounds brilliant," Cora said with obvious relief.

The day was warm, that kind of summer heat when it's hot but just shy of the point of discomfort. It felt top notch to be kinda balmy and sense the rays heating my hair and cooking my complexion. The dry heat helps tremendously too, it sounds like an old wives' tale but, as someone who's traveled more than his reasonable share, I can tell you it's not. I recalled to Cora my periods in the upper East and in portions of the Northwest and how the dampness chilled my bones, even in the dead of summer.

Quickly enough I transported us out to Warnego, a town truly in the middle of nowhere. It was remote but a fairly short drive, sparking my mind to believe that at one point this city stood for something. I parked close to the train tracks, worry free, as cars evidently hadn't powered through here any time recently.

"How do you know we won't encounter any cars?" Cora's concern exceeded my own but, with this, I could astound her.

"Well you can tell by looking at the tracks that no one has been or will be passing through today. Just look." We hopped eagerly out of the car to pursue the investigation.

"Aren't the tracks always rusty, the wooden frame rotted, some bolts missing? This isn't uncustomary."

"Yes, I grant you that, dear. Very impressive, young sleuth," I smarted to Cora in my best, phony French accent. She tittered adorably and awaited my proclamation on the question at hand. "What you need to examine," I began, thrilled for finally unearthing something with which I could match the young lady's wits, "are the sand deposits around and in the middle of the tracks. That build up means that trains aren't passing over--"

"Ohhh…"

"Surprising isn't it?"

"Makes sense."

"Sure. Well…" I was out. *That was all I could say to sound smart? Ugh.*

"Anyway," she flirted.

"Anyway."

"How do you think that boxcar got left there?"

"I don't know," I replied, spinning around, following the motion of Cora's pointed finger.

We paused in silence and the muted desolation of our surroundings matched the lack of conversation between us. It was a pleasant calm, unmistakably, and this was precisely the sort of outing that we needed.

"It's very lonely here, in an odd way," Cora at last uttered.

"Yes. I suppose it is. That's catching for you to think of that," I smiled.

"Suppose so," she whispered.

"You know, I think on occasion about people. People I don't even know. Just young men, old men of this country who had jobs and probably lived around here and each and every time they saw a train bursting through on these tracks they grinned and thought 'heck yeah, the prosperity's finally comin' my way!' but little did they know it was here-and-gone before they knew it."

"I think about it too. Who knew this could happen to us? And now it's a ghost town, Warnego, such a waste."

"Right."

"I reckon just too many people got involved in starting railroads and it went bust. Just overloaded the country."

"Mmm...uh huh." I shuffled my way towards the boxcar and Cora instinctively followed.

"Whatcha doin'?"

"Don't know. Thinkin'. Walkin'. Gonna sit in that boxcar."

"K."

We scurried over and I motioned for Cora to stop abruptly.

"I don't want you to get hurt again. You'd better let me check it out before you come aboard."

"Alright," she smiled in full appreciation of the gesture.

After a thorough examination I decided we would be safe within the empty, iron carcass.

"All aboard!"

Cora laughed rowdily, clutched my extended hand, and sprung onto the boxcar. We situated ourselves on the center of the floor, still close enough to the loading door to feel the sun and vague breeze. And then we did little else but talk, talk, and kiss. All the while we chewed the fat Cora clawed both my hands with each of hers as though she longed to pin me down and prevent misplacing me.

"What do you consider the darkest day of your life?" Her questions were nearly always profound, meaningful, deeply insightful.

"There's a lot to choose from," I nervously laughed. "I suppose I'd say it was just all of those nights when I'd have nowhere to go, nowhere to sleep, and no one to think to turn to. I can't describe what it felt like. At first, you're strong and you suffer through it. Then the humdrum of it all sets in and you're numb. But there comes a point for each of us rail-riders that you think 'is this really my life? To be alone? To sleep on a dirty floor that doesn't even belong to me? To contribute absolutely nothing to our society?' It messes with you. It depresses a man especially. I think ladies would be more scared, although I don't know who would let a woman ever go hungry and sleep out in the raw weather. But…for me, it was the emptiness, the loneliness, and, mostly, the helplessness of it. I absolutely hate feeling helpless. I wanted so much Cora to pick myself up, find a job, and get myself on the right track to being a decent man, but everything was against me—the Depression, and the way most people glare at me."

"Yes. You think there would be more compassion. Or, at minimum, they'd be more used to seeing it."

"Exactly…Let's not get down with all of my sad stories."

"Oh, it's alright. I asked the question, I wanted to know."

"Ok then."

We proceeded in sharing dark moments but nevertheless it was pleasurable and remedying. Maybe it was the sunlight that detached what otherwise could have been a threatening vibe within the conversation. Who's to say? In that moment, I can assure you I cared little about the reasons why things were going so well between Cora and me. I only regarded that they were.

"You know something?" I declared to Cora with the grandest of confidence I'd ever embodied.

"What's that?"

"I truly love you, girl."

"I know. And I love you too."

Whoever said if something seems too good to be true, it probably is, was a fool. And he certainly never knew my Cora.

13

That night surpassed all others previously. Cora and I slept in the boxcar, under the stars, nestled tightly together. It was pitch black with the exception of those luminary masterpieces, not one city light hovering above us or one car passing by for hours on end. We awoke and as she primped her hair and straightened her clothes I jetted to the car to grab some lukewarm cider and a couple bananas.

"Breakfast!" I shouted, hoisting the finds above my head on my walk back.

"Aww, thank you! That is really sweet of you to think of such a thing. First, sandwiches and sodas for supper, then a slice of pie to share as a snack, and now, breakfast to boot. What do you got, a grocery store hidden in that car?"

I laughed, hypnotized as usual by her sweet mockery.

"No, no, not a grocery store. Just enough to get us by. Care to explore a tad more of the land today?" I realized I needed to ask, girls typically were limited on interest when it came to harebrained search-and-find missions.

"Of course, I'm up for it!" Again, Cora's not your conventional girl. *Now, the blood is really rushing in me.*

"So, I thought we could go snoop around that other abandoned car."

"That one over there?" Cora peered off about a thousand feet in the distance.

"It's not a long walk."

"No. I know. I guess I just like our car." Her apprehension confused me but I responded in sustained conviction, as it had been working for me thus far.

"It'll be great Cora. Come on, let's go!"

We traipsed through the sandy, flat earth to our subsequent destination. From the outside this boxcar looked worse for worn: the steel peripheral heavily rusted, dozens of bolts gone astray, graffiti wrapped. Yet, when we slid inside the boxy wreckage it was a different story entirely. One would have thought this car was in use as recently as a month or two prior. With the exception of some dusty sand settling in assorted niches and on the table tops, it was opulent. White plates banked two feet high in the corner, linens atop the cherry eating areas, presumably as napkins and pot-holders, and a few delicate tea cups still perched under cabinets, thanks to a number of tarnished gold hooks.

We strolled through our transportation museum and in marvel and wonder we examined every detail of the car and its contents. Respectable silence blanketed Cora and I, and we crossed paths only once in the antiqued dining room. 'Excuse me' was the lone utterance, spoken by Cora as she passed in front of me to peer more closely at the etched chair rail. Easily an hour drifted by before one of us spoke. It seemed strange to hear noise of any sort.

"Um," I cleared my throat, allowing my ears to readjust. "Did you take a look at this?" I motioned towards a pair of carved initials barely visible on a wooden wall panel.

"Yes," she grinned. Each time she beamed so joyfully my mind played a snippet of classical music. "Canon in D Major" and "Fur Elise" were two of my favorites. I don't know what in particular brought this about; only that it hadn't occurred prior to my life with Cora. She dazzled my mind and tickled my wit; it constantly made me recall all of the stories elder gentlemen had told me regarding the amazing changes brought within their souls because of that *one* woman. I used to label it ridiculous. Now I label myself that for ever being this skeptical of the transformative powers of love.

Cora resumed. "Those initials...they are so sweet!"

"Shall I add ours too?"

"No!" she outburst. Ah, just like my girl to not wish to deface private, albeit disposed, property.

"Alright," I cheerfully appeased. "Would you like to have dinner here tonight?"

"Here?" Cora replied confusedly, skimming over her surroundings.

"Yes!"

"How so?" she laughed, hopefully not at me.

"Oh I have my plans." *How about that for melodious bravado?*

"Sure. Whatever you wish...I leave it in your capable hands!"

I exited the boxcar and returned on one last, lengthy walk to my vehicle. I fumbled through my paper bag of non-perishables to ensure there was, in fact, something to eat. A bag of pecans, two apples, half a jug of water, carrots, and rolls. It wasn't necessarily a full, hearty dinner, but it was enough to satisfy and, with a smoky, smoldering fire it would taste comforting and flavorful. Returning to our spot, I was tired and parched but Cora was eager to resume our conversation.

"And what have you brought me this time?"

"Oh, some vegetable and fruit. Rolls. Good thing is I got a handful or two of pecans also." I dumped a mouthful of water straight from the jug down my throat. I construed Cora considered it uncouth but, thankfully, she made not one remark.

"Well, sounds good."

"It doesn't sound like much but I'm going to make something special for you."

"Aww, that's tender, Jonathan. You must really want to be with me, huh?"

"Yes. Of course. Yes. I'm trying to keep you forever, here."

"No. That's what I'm trying to do."

"Um, no. I am!"

Laughter. Then my cooking preparations began. I halved the apples and scooped out the seeds and core as best I could. Setting them aside, I decided I'd roll them in the pecan crumbs at the bottom of the bag before placing them in the fire. Once my heat was burning strong and steady I crisped the pecans in a handcrafted pan of foil. They toasted quickly and their oils released, coating the foil, allowing the carrots to bake without drying out. I checked the vegetables constantly, worried they could end up too crisp or just mush. As close as to perfection as I might roast them, they were removed from the heat and set aside for plating.

I dusted off each white plate for Cora and I and stacked two small hills of carrots in the center. Next, I sprinkled the pecans atop and all around and they made the most adorable tinkling as they dropped against the china. It was astonishing that I should even notice such a thing, as I was nervously edgy by the responsibility of dinner preparation.

"Shall I sit?" Cora asked. She had pinned the sides of her hair back and reapplied her rouge and lip gloss.

"Yes, pet. My, you look lovely."

"Thank you, sir."

I raised both plates in my hands then I had a finer idea. I set mine back down on the butler top and carried only Cora's serving to the dining table. Coming up from behind her I slowly placed the meal in front of her and whispered 'enjoy' in her ear.

"Thanks," she barely let out, looking in my eyes with her teary ones, our faces mere inches apart.

"You're welcome," I mouthed in return and then lightly kissed her lips. I nabbed my own plate and then sat across from my girl. She was waiting for me to start. "Go ahead and eat, hon," I said.

"Shall we say grace first?"

Speechless, then, "ok." I was nervous, what would I say?

But then Cora reached out her hands and mine fell into hers. She bowed her head, closed her eyes, and I followed her lead. She began the prayer and it permitted the meal to seem even more homemade and exceptional, like Christmas Eve dinner. When grace concluded we paused in comforting silence, gazing at one another with love and warmth.

"That was wonderful, thank you," I choked out.

"We're family, Jonathan."

I stirred within. "Yes!" I agreed. "I know I don't need anybody else."

"Me either," she jollied.

We ate our meal properly, overturned forks, small bites cut precisely, the dabs of linen napkins and all.

"Delectable!" Cora asserted.

"Are you ready for dessert?"

"Wow and dessert to boot? You really did think this through!"

"I try," I teased. I slid the foil from the simmering fire, wishing passionately that the apples would be visibly intact and wouldn't taste like carrots or burned aluminum. "I crave some ice cream or whipped topping, looking at these apples!"

"Well they smell delicious, as is!"

Turns out they were.

"I can't tell you enough how I truly appreciate the meal."

"Oh, you're very welcome Cora. It was a pleasure to do and it extended our day so were able to spend more time together."

"Ahh, so that was your reasoning behind it."

"Of course," I toyed.

"Well I had the best of times."

"Me, too."

We parted soon thereafter, following our best attempts at washing our dishes, replacing each cup and platter to its prior location, and ensuring the fire was fully out and buried.

It had been a night to remember, indeed. It was my first impression of what could be my future life, my family, built with Cora, and it was unmistakably impressive.

14

Walking through town on another sunny piercingly-bright afternoon overwhelmed me with pleasure. Cora had a hop in her step and I wondered what had created it.

"Shall I ask why you're so happy or shall I simply enjoy it?" I grinned.

"Enjoy it...and ask!" she returned.

"Ok, darlin', so then tell me."

She pirouetted around on her ivory heel, arms fully spread, smile breaking forth, eyes twinkling in the rays.

"You're such a tease!"

"I am not a tease," she insisted poorly, "I am a slowpoke, maybe, but that's all."

I hastily nabbed her right wrist as she spun before me again, and halted the ballerina. It appeared to have angered her.

"Sorry. I just wanted to look at you when we were speaking."

The firmness in her face broke. "Oh, ok then. My apologies."

"No, it's alright, you don't have to apologize," I blushed. *How is this turning into an uncomfortable episode?*

"Don't worry about it," she laughed it off. Then, she shrugged and said, "No problems, tell me whatever you want."

"Oh." My mind drew a blank; all the commotion had wiped it clean.

"Alright then!" she cheered. "*I* shall think of something to talk about."

"K." Relief.

"Did you see that family we passed earlier?"

"Sure."

"Well, what did you think? I mean, what went through your mind in seeing them?"

"I don't know. Let's see…they looked pretty happy and all. A nice, middle-American family."

"Go on."

"I'd guess they're on their way to an early supper. Probably early risers, the father's a farmer; his wife, a homemaker; the eldest boy, a fine chap who helps his share and then some 'round the farm; the younger one, jolly and mostly hardworking too; and, the girl, well she's the dreamer. The daughter had an intense look in her eyes, something I've seen before," I peered over at Cora. "Like she's always thinking. She'll grow up, leave the farm, her family, this town, to venture off to big city life and the university. I'd reckon she will make the most of her talents and desires and meet a rich fellow and few around her will ever realize *this* is where she came from."

"Yes!" Evidently she was impressed by my once-over.

"Don't know, could be wrong," I inserted my best attempt at humility. "But I doubt it!"

"What?!" she rolled in jubilation. "And how are you so sure may I ask?" Cora's sarcasm, always keenly endearing.

"Because of you. That young girl, she's who you once were." I stated it with every ounce of confidence I had remaining. Cora did not confirm the validity of my estimation but even in her silence she spoke volumes. Her eyes penetrated through my mind as though her only means of informing me I was right was through subconscious communication.

Finally she said, "Well this place isn't so bad."

"No?" I gently inquired.

"No. Kansas. It's actually a beautiful place. I don't get why I'm the only one to acknowledge that."

"Because you see the good that others don't."

"Thanks. But, honestly, what is so wrong with Kansas?"

"Cora, there's no opportunity here. That's all."

"Well I disagree. The opportunities exist here they are just different or less obvious. Haven't you ever heard, 'The light at the end of the tunnel is just the light of an oncoming train'?"

"No, I haven't. It makes sense though."

"Of course it does." And with that she held my hand and swiftly strolled at my pace through town. I kept noticing Cora staring at me out of the right corner of my eye. I failed to acknowledge it, not because it made me uncomfortable or because it ceased to impress me, but, rather, I had grown accustomed to it. Finally I decided to change the subject and ask Cora to elaborate on her current readings.

"Yes, I'm still reading *Look Homeward, Angel.*"

"It's a long one, huh?"

"Yes, it is, but I'm truly enjoying it!"

"Uh-huh. And who is the angel intended to look homeward?"

"Very remarkable question, Johnny!"

Giggles. "You know I love when you call me that!"

"Yeah…well, let's see. It's not so much who it is but rather just the idea of home, what is represents for each of us and Wolfe does an incredible job of showing the dark side of it, too."

"I can't fathom home ever being negative, you know?"

"True. But then again, think of how it could be. What if you have real trials in your family—which everyone does—but you really experience some horrific things and your way of dealing with them is to write about them, to tell them to the world, and then your home rejects you because they see it as a betrayal."

I shook my head in disbelief. "I've never thought of that before."

"It's something Wolfe explored and I considered it incredulous that someone could punish a friend, a relative, even a townsperson, just for being honest."

"I agree. You will have to keep telling me about the novel, it sounds captivating."

"You should read it with me!"

"Ha, I don't think I'm ready for a reading that substantial yet!"

"Ok…Maybe a short story then?"

"K, sure. Anything in mind?"

"Well Wolfe's writing *God's Lonely Man* is a good one."

"You've read it before?"

"Only once. It really spoke to me and I'd love to see how it affects you."

"It sure has a provocative title."

"Well, he certainly is captivated by the concept of loneliness. I think many of us are, it's such a common—miserable—experience."

"Uh huh."

"Actually I've also seen it under the title of *The Anatomy of Loneliness*, appropriately enough."

"Hmm."

"Yeah. So--"

"So--"

"I think that we're having quite a productively conversational day today," she overjoyed.

"Me too," I amused.

"Can I ask you something?" she resumed in a more serious tone.

"Of course, whatever you'd like."

"What do you think about when you think about your family?"

"Pain, mostly. And some confusion as well."

"Confusion?"

"Yes, I'm confused why they have behaved as they have…non-committal, distant, disinterested."

"Right."

"I try not to think about them honestly."

"But you must, I expect."

"Sure, yet I know there is little I can do. But live my life in any way that I can, alone or not."

"You are not alone, Jonathan."

"Thanks to you, I am not alone. And I sincerely hope that it stays this way."

"It will," she chuckled, "if you want it to."

"I do."

"I do too."

Magnificently, we sounded extraordinarily *committed*. The weekend was proving as much; it would be simply the first of many, many comparable days.

15

Walking through town that weekend we encountered a pair of familiar, friendly faces. It was the Smiths and indubitably a delight to see them once more.

"Why, hello!" Mrs. Smith cheered.

"Hello, ma'am," I replied.

Cora and Mr. Smith chimed in as well and we proceeded to cover all expected topics of the moment: the healing of Cora's wounds, the weather, the ever-deepening depression, and then, the Smith's annual barn dance and get-together. We were invited, no, commanded to come and I retorted rapidly that Cora and I would most certainly be present.

Hastily the quartet of us was necessitated to say our goodbyes, for the Smiths had several errands to complete and family business to attend to that evening.

"It was wonderful to meet up with them, huh?" Cora mentioned.

"Yes dear," I sweetly countered.

"Do you think we'll be like that one day?"

"Like what?" I inquired, with only minimal need for clarification.

"Like the Smiths."

I blathered. "Of course, that's whom I thought you were talking about! How so?"

"Well they appear to be genuinely happy and they completely embody that, I don't know, *togetherness* that all marriages should have."

"They do."

"But will that be *us*?" she posed again.

"I'm sure of it, sunshine."

Doubtlessly this pleased Cora and commenced our afternoon off to the best possible start.

"Great!" she sung. "What would you like to do now honey?"

"Let's get some ice cream."

"Ooh! Yes, let's."

Pausing briefly at Holtz's menu board we each selected the flavor of our choosing and then ordered single-scoop cones.

"How's your Dutch chocolate, Jonathan?"

"Good. Great. You like your pineapple vanilla?"

"Not really. Let's swap!"

I froze in motion and mentioning.

"Um," I thought. Then I glanced at Cora's puppy-dog eyes and curled lower lip, and I caved. "Sure, sweetheart."

We exchanged cones and fortunately enough for me the pineapple vanilla tasted better than it sounded and looked. The pineapple was tart and sweet, the vanilla full-flavored and extra creamy. It was delightful and I consumed it all, however, not as rapidly as Cora devoured hers.

"Delicious!" she announced to me and the strangers passing by. They smiled in admiration of her youthful, exuberant nature.

"Yes, you are," I flirted. Cora blushed and her rosy cheeks served as a gorgeous front to the backdrop of plush clouds, aqua sky, and rays of buttery sunlight.

"You're really *so* nice," she complimented.

"Thanks." I brushed it off. "And now what are your ideas for the day?"

"Oh I do have one," she surprised me.

"Yeah? What's that?"

"Come. Let's sit."

We parked ourselves at a worn wooden bench which, despite their age and disrepair, so beautifully filled the downtown streets.

"Sitting on a bench, a clever move," I teased.

"I'm just getting started," she flirted in return.

Cora reached deep into her lavender satchel and retrieved a tiny, black hardcover book. She whipped it out as though it were a white rabbit and the satchel a magician's top hat.

"Ooh," I said, in masculine confidence.

"Your anticipation, please."

"You have it dear."

"I purchased this from Morgan's Pharmacy in town--"

"Uh-huh--"

"It's," she began to bellow and hoot uncontrollably.

"What?" I laughed, it was contagious I suppose.

"It's," she continued, "it's called a tea book."

She composed herself.

"Oh a book on making tea or teas of the world?" It was a fair guess. A wrong one, yet, and it set off her cackles again.

"No, sweetheart," she clarified in nearly a condescending tone. "It's a book of questions, for fun alone, you can pose to a friend… over a cup of tea, they say."

"Ahh."

"Would you like to give it a try?"

"Sure I'll give it a go. Whatever you desire."

"K." With fierce enthusiasm Cora flung the book open, just about breaking the binding. "Alright, first question!"

I withstood the urge to laugh at her thrill for the forthcoming interrogation.

"What is your dream job?"

"Pilot."

"Ok, question two, how many children do you wish to have?"

"Four."

"Great. Third question. And feel free to elaborate if you'd like. Where in the world would you most like to visit?"

I thought, perplexed. After a few moments, "Australia."

"Really?"

"Sure."

"Why is that?"

"I dunno. I just think it sounds like an incredible land from what I've heard about it. It's there, on the other side of the world all by itself. There's so much to it too, you know? There are forests, beaches, deserts, pretty much all that any of us could imagine encountering on an adventure. And I would just be this traveler wandering through, exposing myself to all the different animals, snakes, plants, food, what-have-you."

"Wow, you make it sound good…except for the snakes."

"Yeah," I conceded. "Well what about you? Shouldn't you be answering these questions also?"

"Oh I don't have to," she modestly replied.

"You *are* an intriguing person, Cora."

"Really?" The expression on her face was one of downright astonishment.

"Heck, yeah! How…how do you not know this already?"

"I don't know," she self-deprecated. Her hands wrung one another habitually and she uncomfortably repositioned herself several times.

"Cora, I can't even fathom why you haven't been told a thousand times before that you are amazing—the most amazing, astonishing, gorgeous inside and out, classy woman in the state of Kansas. But trust me, you are."

"Thanks so much!" Her glow immediately returned and in spite of everything she managed to pervade my ego, thanking me several more times.

"I can't get over how much we've bonded, Cora."

"Me too!" She sprung up in excitement and dashed over, to atop my lap, her arms squeezing forcefully around my neck, her shrieking voice buried close to my right ear.

"Wow you can do that anytime!"

"*Ha ha*, I know I shouldn't, we're in public, but I couldn't resist! Do you have any idea how happy you're making me?!"

"Cora, you're on my lap, clutching my shirt collar, I think I know."

Hilarity persists. A few minutes afterward she popped up brightly and yanked me to my feet, all but removing my arms from their sockets.

"Whoa, gal," I had just about landed on my derrière, compliments of her forcefulness. "I never knew such a little thing could harness that kind of power!"

"It pays not to underestimate me, mister."

"I guess not," I toyed.

And she could not have been more right. I wondered what surprise would be coming to me next, courtesy of Cora's cleverness.

16

At home that evening Cora lived up to my expectations. She floated around her room, setting up her bed with paper, a ruler, a black fountain pen set, pencils, a white ink-stained rag, and the instrument of her current choosing, a used, damaged Bergonzi violin. In actuality, she was a piano girl, but there wasn't one roundabout.

"I hope this still sounds tolerable," she fretted to herself.

Perched atop her creaking, coiled mattress she fumbled with the pencils and paper sheets, and then doodled away as her inner voice emerged. Frantically the ideas came to her, as they always did, and she scribbled almost illegibly on the blank pages. Twenty minutes or fewer passed and all of the lyrics were complete. It was a love story and now, for the arduous part, she would compose the accompaniment. Always, she began with the melody. It was knowingly essential and, therefore, of great stress to Cora to pick suitable notes. Though not a singer herself, songs were created to be sung and, thus, she had to force her composer mind to consider such obviousness.

Perching the violin back against her shoulder and the chin rest under her tiny jaw, Cora clutched the neck with her left hand and slithered her fingers slowly down the strings, ensuring the tuning pegs were appropriately adjusted. As the bow graced the gut strings she closed her eyes, listening for proper timbre. Once satisfied she proceeded to try out a variety of note sequences to select the fitting melody for Jonathan's song. This process alone often took hours and required the visionary's total concentration and emotional dedication.

Several hours passed and the once-white pages, now a mute grey-tone smeared with soft pencil graphite, were flooded with words, letters, and fractions denoting the length of each note. She had also supplemented with accompanying chords and the beginnings of a bass line. Struggling with the bass line was nothing new to Cora; for every song it was her paramount challenge. Indeed, one would consider it remarkable that she continued to compose, considering her loathing of the formation of the rhythmic pulse.

Early that evening the tune was complete.

"I think that's the quickest I ever wrote one!" she pleased herself with the congratulations.

Regardless of her fatigue and worn mind Cora finished one final task, the most important, the purpose. She seized her ruler and laid it stringently on fresh white paper. With the delicate hands of an architect she drew the lines to construct her own staff paper. It was an exquisite, intricate process, but something she quite enjoyed. Cora's eye for detail and meticulousness was splendid, and the task suited her compulsive nature quite well. Upon the drying of the sheets she filled in every measure with all of the needed notes, clearly wrote the corresponding lyrics underneath, and finished with a title, date, and signing. The piece, called "There Goes My Heart," imparted every one of her most passionate and acute feelings for Jonathan.

The impetuosity to deliver it to him was overwhelming, but she paced the room, cleaned up, and paced the room again, until the sheets were dry enough to be handled. An hour later, they were. Cora positioned a piece at a time against the gold background of the large frame she retrieved. After all six sheets were in place and secured to the back board, she covered the front with a cumbersome piece of glass, reattached the sides of the frame, and taped on a homemade bow using one of her red hair ribbons. She tipped the frame slightly against her bed, stood back, and peered at it for a brief time. More than anything else, she admired it because it conveyed what was in her heart and that was the true motivation for this artist, or any other.

The span it took Cora to transport and deliver the frame is not important. It was lengthy nonetheless because of the weight and delicacy of the gift. Still, she arrived at the boardinghouse, frame in tow, and asked the keeper to place it at Jonathan's room. She gladly obliged, leaned it gently against his door, and the song was awaiting his return that dusk.

When I arrived, I scarcely knew what to say. A huge, polished picture frame at my doorstep, the antique finished border, the golden background, and the immaculate glass. Yet, it was what lay underneath that enveloped me. I could not read music but I could immediately note the effort and the ardor that went into such a masterpiece. It was stunning, both in meaning and execution. The tiny oval notes so perfectly filled in, all the clefs and names-I-don't-know symbols flawlessly rounded, each word printed as painstakingly as a press's. But once I actually stopped the physical admiration of the gift and read it thoroughly, attempting to feel the notes as best as a layman could, my heart surged with joy and gratitude. How could a woman love me this much? I didn't know, but I wanted more than anything else for it to never end.

"What's that, my good man?" It was Ralph Anderson, an unemployed writer who was traveling across the Dust Bowl. He had been staying at the house for about two weeks and we had taken to enjoying each other's conversations.

Speechless.

"A gift from your girl?"
"Yes. How did you know?"
"By the look on your face," he amused.
I can't imagine how I must have looked.

17

*C*ora and I walked into Smiths' barn and were equally delighted and nervous. It was well-lit and the tiny white lights sparkled against the waxed wood floor. Bundles of hay served as easy chairs for chatters and resting dancers. It smelled of sweet pine and warm, roasted hors d'oeuvres and my eye repeatedly glanced at the barbeque sandwiches Joanna Smith constructed at a far picnic table. A handful of children gathered around to observe her generously amassing tender pork atop the freshly baked rolls and whipping a dollop of honey and thick barbeque sauce over each.

Spring-clad couples danced joyfully to "Buttons and Bows" and as I watched young men hold the waistline and gently grip the hand of the woman they each loved, it occurred to me that I should ask Cora to dance. But my bravery hadn't caught up with my appetite just yet.

"What do you want to do?" Cora asked me through her mincing chuckles.

"What's so funny, doll?"

"Nothin'."

"Oh, sure, right," I beamed. "Tell me, what is it?"

"I can't tell if you look confused or happy, Jonathan!" Her eyes twinkled and her smile spread so panoramically that I assumed it must have made her cheeks sore.

"You look beautiful, beautiful." Never had I sounded so sanguine and certain.

"Jonathan…" Cora glimpsed towards the floor and shuffled a piece of hay with the tip of her left shoe. It was palpable that my compliment embarrassed her.

"I didn't mean to make you blush. Don't worry, it happens to me all the time around you, doesn't it?" For the first time I felt qualified at being the right man in Cora's life who would be able to protect her and reassure her every moment. She slid her meager wrist under my elbow and grabbed hold of my upper arm, and as she clutched my suit jacket I could tell she was clinging on for dear life.

I peered deeply into her eyes with a nearly-tense seriousness that would be unrecognizable to her.

"Don't ever let go," I demanded.

Cora smiled in compliance.

Joanna and Gary Smith paused from hostess and host duties and proudly traipsed to the dance floor, hand in hand. Oblivious to the eyes upon them, they centered on one another and left their guests to fend for themselves. I could see in the focused visages their devotion to each other and I longed to point it out to Cora as if to say, *look that's what I want us to become.* Yet, I concluded it difficult to speak because my mind panicked itself and I wondered if I was headed towards an ending like the Smiths, or was this simply make-believe? I always fathomed it unrealistic that couples culminated into one true, deliriously happy being but, then again, let us not forget my life that has been nearly drowned in negativity and loneliness. Cora could be, after all, the one to change everything. The end of me *could be* a man who finds joy in working hard to provide for his family, who is fortunate to come home to a loyal woman every night, who is able to chart his successes and relish in them as he hosts the townspeople for an anticipated occasion; a man who is another Gary Smith. *Am I?*, I thought.

Something must have shown upon my face to reflect my inner dialogue because Cora blurted abruptly, "What's wrong?"

She had distress in her voice like I had never antecedently encountered. But I couldn't muster the fortitude inside to conceal my thoughts and doubts, so I neglected even the courtesy of a reply. Cora stood motionless, her green eyes widely positioned, her soft pink lips frozen in a gasp.

"Jonathan." Even in only uttering my name she requested a response.

Two solitary tears slinked down my cheeks and I realized I was transparent.

"Jonathan...what...is wrong?" I could feel her heart race with my eyes alone. *Say something, damn fool, don't do this to her.*

"I need air," I spat the words out as I dashed away from Cora, through the felicitous crowd, and under the horse rails to a desolate part of Smiths' wheat field. *Breathe. Breathe.* I was ingesting air so vigorously that I was close to vomiting or hyperventilating.

I bent forward, my head immersing with blood and swinging between my knees. I choked on the air I had excessively devoured and profusely sweated around my collar and chest. My forehead was pounding from the tension and heat and I considered it impossible to regain my composure, let alone my ability to reenter the dance. My mind attempted to wonder about Cora; *was she alright? was she angry?*, but I was too out-of-sorts to coherently draw conclusions.

I plopped onto the wet grass and sat stock-still. As moments passed I began to poise myself; first, wiping the sweat from my brow; next, finger combing my hair; then, smoothing my shirt and slacks. I did nothing but breathe unhurriedly in those minutes. *When the time comes, I will be able to resolve this,* I expected.

Unsure of how much time had passed I arose and commenced shuffling back to the barn. I prayed that I could well-disguise my episode and convince Cora to forget my lapse in proper judgment. As

I neared the weathered doors I heard one of my favorite tunes, "Show Me the Way to Go Home," by Vincent Lopez. The song suited me so well, a misfit who makes the wrong choices and attempts to soothe mistakes with vices like drinking. All I wanted, like the man himself said, was to go home after a long night. And when I saw Cora I thought, *home, I am.*

18

ust then, Cora flipped me the oddest look. I could tell she was
angry or, at the least, disappointed in my behavior.

"Hi," I uttered. I couldn't imagine what else to say.

"Hi," she replied sounding deflated and disheartened.

"Look, I'm sorry about that."

"Uh-huh."

"No, really, I am. If you'd let me, I'll explain."

No response.

"Ok?"

"I'm listening." She crossed her arms, tightened her lips, and
peered down at my shoes.

"Cora, sometimes I have difficulty dealing with things, like how
marvelous you are--"

"Oh, come on," she said disgusted.

"No, I am not being coy here. Truly, I get caught up sometimes
and then I realize I can have it all but, even knowing that, I still
allow hopelessness from the past to affect me and--"

"And it's going to ruin the good thing we have."

"I know. I don't want that."

She paused momentarily as though she wanted to be certain of
publicizing her response.

"No, I don't want that either, Jonathan. Come here."

She extended her hands towards me and I wanted to fall within her frail arms. Somehow they didn't seem frail in this instance but rather reflective of the strength of a young woman on the verge of wifedom and motherhood. As enticed as I was to go to her warm bosom I instantaneously resolved to accept another course.

My hands cupped her diminutive chin and my fingers welded to her supple, blushing cheeks. Easily I drew her near and pressed my chapped lips to her own. Anon I could taste her fruity lip balm and the fresh mint from the tea she had been drinking. It was more romantic of a kiss than I had expected I could pull off, which isn't to imply that it was long-lasting. Cora was a gentle lady and I dared not attempt anything in public which may fetch her criticism. When I let go and she fell back leisurely as though easing onto a cloud, I could see in her eyes that it had not been a mistake. For once, my luck was changing.

We passed the rest of the night chatting with other guests and dancing gleefully like young, elated lovers. The cheer in her eyes as I dosey-doed with Britney Portman, the six-year-old daughter of the Smiths' neighbors, was unforgettable. I treasured this evening because I comprehended that it was one of those once-in-a-lifetime occurrences. Cora and I had faced a trial together and, not only had we survived, we were now bonded and blissful.

The following day I was expecting to hear from Cora, as we had agreed upon plans to picnic in Linscott Park. She didn't telephone and I was perplexed as to how to respond. Certainly, I wanted to avoid forcing myself upon her if it was not her wishes, but how could that be so, given the out-of-this-world preceding night? I lingered at home, restlessly passing the time until she would call but, alas, she did not. I was more worried than anything and repeatedly hoped that whatever had transpired was neither severe nor anguished. Eventually the day was over and, still, no communication from Cora.

A knock at my door.

"Hello," I muttered while slowly opening it, assuming incorrectly that it was a fellow tenant. It was Cora.

"Hi."

I said nothing.

"I said 'hi'."

"Hey."

"Don't be rude."

"Rude?" *Is she freakin' kidding me?* "You're one to talk. Where the hell have you been?"

"Excuse me?"

"You heard me. Now answer the question. *Now*, Cora."

"I won't be addressed in such a tone."

"Whatever then, goodnight." I quickly closed the door. A minute later there was a second knock. "What can I do for you?" I said amidst its reopening.

"This is very shocking behavior, Jon--"

"Not as shocking as yours!" And for the second time, the door slammed shut.

"Open this door right now! I'm coming in!" Cora ranted while monstrously banging her fist against the wood.

"You're making a scene! Get in here!" For the third and final time, I opened my door, and she confidently strolled in. "What is your problem Cora? I haven't seen or heard from you all…day…long and yet you show up at my residence and immediately start bickering with me? What's that all about? I've never seen you this disrespectful before!"

"Hold on and let me talk, would you?"

"Go ahead." I threw my arms in the air with apparent apathy.

"Oh, well, if you don't care--"

"Cut the sarcasm and just give me an explanation please."

She stood in silence, definitely intimidated and, needless to say, annoyed, by my rarely-seen hard-hitting nature.

"I want something you can't give me. Or won't give me, whichever it is," she whispered with the innocence I recognized from some of our more intimate conversations. I took the sentences in, not sure how to process nor respond to them.

"What does that mean, Cora? What is this *something?*"

"I need to feel secure--"

"And I don't do that?"

"Honestly? No."

"I, I'm shocked, to say the least. The thing, Cora—yeah we can talk about it and all—but I wonder how you can even question *me* about security when you don't even bother to call and let me know you're alive, you're not interested in getting together today, you never want to speak with me again, what-have-you! You can't even call!"

"I'm sorry, alright?"

"No…no it's not alright. I'm not going to excuse this."

Oh yeah, she was speechless.

"I find it preposterous that you want to hold me to a certain standard for which you aren't held. That's nonsense Cora and you know it!"

From the following expressions, teardrops, and eye-rolling, I surmised that the woman had never been placed accountable in such a manner. Don't get me wrong, it pained me to hurt her, but it felt the right thing to do to reprimand both of us or neither at all.

She exhaled noisily, but continued to fail to speak.

"Cora!" I uttered, more to alarm her into talking than to discipline or infuriate her.

Nothing.

19

S he stormed out. And that was it for our evening.

I went to bed, eventually, but how could I sleep? Answers evaded me, as did rest. There were many things I needed to say to Cora, but for the life of me they wouldn't come out.

That same morning Cora darted through town, no destination in mind; she was simply scurrying, scurrying away from Jonathan's insecurities. At a few moments of interrupted love, she nearly paused long enough to forgive him and retrace her steps back to the boardinghouse, but she would not allow herself.

"Don't let him get the best of you," she thought. "This country is full of men of real hunger. True men ready and willing and praying and anxious for a job, a home, a wife, a family. And *he* wants to take his sweet time...for what? The job that he *doesn't* have? His career that is going nowhere? How could he put this upon me? He gives me nothing and I offer him my all--"

In that moment Cora's mind wandered to the worst of possible scenarios. Perhaps Jonathan wasn't predisposed to furthering their commitment because he was interested in the pursuit of the female species and in more than one solitary creature.

"No, it can't be so; I know him," she whispered within.

"Hey gal!"

She sustained her walk.

"Gir-lie!"

It was Pavel, and she knew it the first time around. Hoping to avoid him Cora picked up the pace to one step shy of ferociousness, but with the second calling she had little choice but to pause. If Cora was anything, it was perpetually polite.

"Hi," she quipped.

"Hey," he joked, "where's the fire? I mean, what's the hurry—got a hot date for mornin' flapjacks?" Pavel toiled himself into hysterics.

"No, just out and about," she spoke prettily, plodding away simultaneously.

"Wait, now, where ya going? You can't talk to me for five minutes? I hardly ever see you! Ever since that boy took you away from the world. You know, I knew he'd be no good for you, I knew it all along, in fact I--"

"I—I'm not with him anymore, so not to worry." It killed Cora to choke the words out, and she didn't really believe them anyway. She mouthed them more to wrap up the conversation than to actually address the topic at hand.

"Right! Good! Yeah I figured that. He's with that tart anyway, what's-her-name, I--"

"What?! Who is he with?"

"Whoa! Settle down there Sherlock Holmes. You act like you have something invested here." Cora was in no mood for sarcasm. Funny thing though is Pavel hadn't noticed. "I thought you knew."

"Sure...I mean, I don't who he's seeing but I had expected it was someone. You know."

"Ah. Uh. Uh-huh." Wholly unconvinced Pavel responded, "So if you're wondering he's been seein' Stephanie Binfield, I heard. For a while, I guess."

She motioned the word 'oh' from her lips but no sound emerged. The rest of her face was frozen, as was her body, needless to say.

"You alright, kiddo?" Now, he controlled his humor.

"Yeah. I gotta go, Pavel, sorry." She failed to linger long enough for an acknowledgement or reply. She figured she'd extend her apologies at a forthcoming date, for her brazenness in abruptly parting with Pavel that morning. Tears spurted from her eyes, smearing her rouge into a sticky, sweaty mess. Her top lip clammy from her instantly-running nose, her hair nastily disheveled from the nervous hands racing though them.

Should she see him?

"To find him?" she asked herself through her sickness of weeping. Her legs changing directions every half block to his house, then not, then, then not. She didn't know. She debated.

Then decided.

"Let him go," her inner voice declared.

Three hours later, a visual disaster from head to toe, Cora arrived at home. For once, she pitched her clothes on the floor and haphazardly piled her jewelry on a writing desk. She ripped the bobby pins from her hair that hadn't already fallen out and left them trashed in the porcelain sink, stray hairs and all. She sunk onto her bed and managed to swathe her torso and one leg with the lavender, white, and yellow quilt fashioned by her maternal grandmother. Staring at her crisp eggshell ceiling her eyes searched frantically for flaws within the plaster and paint finish, finding none.

'How could he?' were the only words to travel quietly through her lips before she sobbed herself into a stupor, then asleep. When awakened by a neighbor boy's ball bumping the wooden sill beneath her window, she returned to steeping in this new, pitiless reality. Her mind couldn't make sense of it and it was unambiguous to Cora's conscience that she would have zero peace until she confronted Jonathan directly. Quickly, she dressed in relaxed garb, snatched her clutch from her vanity table, and marched towards his boardinghouse.

With no makeup, no hairstyle, and no preconceived conversation starters, she turned up at the front porch with little more than her poise and her heart in her hands. She halted only to attempt to clear the lump sitting firmly in her throat with a few hearty coughs but, upon the realization that it would not be, she rushed up the stairs and pounded on his door with the meat in her right fist.

Swiftly, he answered.

"Hello?" It was almost as though neither knew even the most elementary words to say.

'Hello' was all she replied, too.

Five minutes passed.

"I'm glad you came," he announced.

"I came here for a conversation."

"Yes, of course," he encouraged, widely opening the door and gesturing with his free arm to enter. "Please. Take a seat if you'd like. I'll get you some tea."

"Thank you." She stepped forth. "Water'll be good." She perambulated towards his bed, precisely placing her clutch near the pillow, and sat at the center of the foot.

"I know--"

"You know nothing," she interrupted.

Silenced, then Jonathan remarked, "Excuse me, sweetheart. You know--"

"Oh apparently I know nothing too."

He paused, eyes roving wildly. "I'm not following you."

"I know about you and Stephanie. You will fool me no more. No man will make a fool of me, Jonathan," she shouted in between the now-present teardrops. "I may be tenderhearted and soft to the eye but I am no dunce. I shall not marry a man, be his wife in the name of God, and turn a blind eye as he gallivants around town. So, if you think I shall, I've come to inform you it will not be so."

"I see." He settled the half-glass of water on the bedside stand

and took a step back. "What can I say Cora but I've never taken you for a fool? I consider you to be the loveliest, most genuine,--"

"Save it."

"No, genuine and, sure enough, intelligent woman I've ever known. I, I'm sorry more than I can say for what I've done wrong." Now the sobs were on his part and they were the most pain-stricken she had thus far witnessed from any man. "Things are definitely over between Stephanie and me. I can tell you that much. *They are I tell you!* I was a jerk, a fool, the biggest clown of them all! You are all I want, or will ever want. Please! Please, I beg you! Forgive me while I can still have the prospect of making it up to you. To repay you in full for my bad choices. I'll make those reparations, I swear to you I will!"

Not a word of reply.

He continued, "Cora, listen to me. I'm telling you as a man would only tell a woman he truly loves. I—I—I wouldn't be here on my knees begging you to keep me in your life if I didn't realize what I had with you! *I see what I stand to lose! I see it all now!* All I want is another chance. Please just one more shot." His soaked head lay upon her lap and his moans only slightly muffled by her knit pants. He was wailing in emotional pain, shuddering and sweating out his own regretful heartache, still beseeching Cora to keep her heart within his contemptible grasp.

Nary a word again.

His begging was relentless. Even on hands and knees he couldn't stop, not one suspension for self-composure. "I'll withhold nothin' from you now on," he bemoaned. "I'll make whatever changes got to be made. Do what's got to be done. Do what you say! Please, I'll do it all. I'll do it all. I'll do it all. I'll--"

His hands clutched together, the joints white from lack of blood flow, the wrists cemented to the surrounding bones, not an inch of movement. Finally, she peered down upon him, more so in pity than in aversion, and said, "Alright...I'll take the chance."

20

$\mathcal{E}$ ach day thereafter Cora and I were inseparable. We were making the effort that both of us should have been making all along. I couldn't help but believe that we would be unstoppable if our feet were held to the fire, especially mine. I think Cora always made considerable efforts; I just yearned desperately for her to gather more patience with me. Admittedly, I wasn't always a gentleman, a provider, a good listener. This would take time and I prayed she was willing to offer that much.

I must say, one particular evening was markedly unforgettable. We met on New York Avenue at midnight. Yes that old familiar street that had connected us, awkwardly or not, in the beginning of our relationship.

This is what happened...

It was eleven o'clock and she appeared uncomfortably rushed when she had at last arrived.

"You still had nearly another hour," I affirmed.

"I know, I'm just not a last minute kind of girl," she kidded.

"Yes, I know, Cora!"

Our spirits were eminently jovial and I promptly surmised that there would be something fantastically atypical about said evening.

"I am so excited!" she overjoyed. "Now that I'm here I can finally grow giddy on our plans! I've brought the chocolates and sparkling cider…did you bring the sandwiches and a book?"

"Of course."

"Great!" I hadn't previously witnessed Cora *this* amused. She bubbled over, nearly tripping amidst her own two feet. Hopping and spiraling, shrieking and smiling, she oozed what every man wanted to behold: happiness simply in his presence.

Only a few minutes passed, all occupied by Cora's glee and jabber, and then, most monstrously and dreadfully unpredicted, our plans were thrown for a loop. It started to downpour, inundating the streets with a drench, bone chilling and soul sopping. There was truly nowhere to go.

"Here!" I commanded to Cora. "At least you can stand under the marquee."

She huddled under the overhanging, curling herself at peculiar angles against the exterior wall in a feeble crack to save her already sodden clothes.

"What about you?" she blustered.

"It's fine," I hollered back, already doused, my eyes scarcely squinting from the pellets shooting at my face.

"I'm soaked too," she whined, her eyes vaguely pink from what I assumed were tears of disappointment.

"I know…it's alright, we'll still think of something to do," I reassured my girl as best as I could. True, I could visibly perceive my words were of little value, but I had to make the effort regardless.

We stood in the shower for at least thirty minutes; it was grisly, approaching ungodly. Then, just before midnight, it abruptly stopped. The sky was black, we were in awe, and Cora's tears were now in plain sight.

"No need to cry, darlin'."

"I know," she sniffled. "But it's ruined…our plans…our night…what was supposed to be a great evening! It's all ruined!

The chocolates, the cider, the walk down the avenue, it's shattered completely!"

"Yeah who knows where those sandwiches are," I joked, glancing around at my previous standing spot. "Oh I think that's them in that puddle over yonder."

"It's not funny! We planned this to be something special."

"It still can be."

She glared, bewildered.

"Come here." I extended my arm and smiled sedately. I waited until her soft hand gripped my own. Pulling her inches from me, I dabbed raindrops off of her forehead, meagerly fixing her hairdo in the process.

Our eyes locked.

"*I can't give you anything but love, baby. That's the only thing I've plenty of, baby. Dream a while, scheme a while. You're sure to find, happiness and I guess…All those things you've always pined for.*" My singing stunk. But it was a miraculous turn. We began to slow-dance, and I carried on. "*Now, gee I love to see you lookin' swell, baby. Diamond bracelets Woolworth doesn't sell, baby. Till that lucky day, you know darn well, baby. I can't give you anything but love.*" I stopped; our eyes still locked; I said, "Well, I can't."

"I love that song. And I love you."

I'm tellin' ya, she meant it. A man just knows.

"We can still have the chocolates," she said. "They're maybe a little melted, but I bet still delicious." She schlepped the lunch-sized brown bag from her coat pocket and removed a small gold foil box. She slid off the loose bow, lifted the lid, and examined the contents inside. "Well, don't look too appetizing, but shall we give 'em a try?"

"Heck yeah."

Laughter; then the sound of water droplets skipping off roof tops onto window panes and aluminum drain spouts. Cora delicately removed a chocolate piece and slowly raised it to my lips. She hesitated before it touched my tongue and rushed it to her exposed grin.

"Mmm…yummy!" she overjoyed like an adolescent. She ardently masticated the half piece, her eyes closing and emerging, her focus spellbound on the creamy dark chocolate and its rich caramel and cocoa interior. Licking her lips after finally swallowing she needlessly posed the question, 'wanna try a piece?'

"Yes, please." *Keep it polite.*

Cora propelled the other half of the treat into my mouth and I immediately related to her look of savory indulgence mere seconds prior. Before I finished chewing the sugary delight, I partook in another indulgence—Cora's lips pressed against my own.

"Why thank you," I coughed out while swallowing the remaining tastes.

"Anytime!" she smiled.

"Today has been great, hasn't it?"

"Yes! Remarkable!" she overjoyed.

"I feel truly blessed that everything is going well between us now."

"Me too. You say that though like it may end."

"Oh, of course not darlin'."

"K."

"I don't know what life holds in store for us but as long as we're together, we'll manage and get through it all."

"Definitely! I think though, Jonathan, that you should reconsider what I've told you previously—you need to take hold of the dreams you have and pursue them."

"Really?"

"Well, why not?"

"I don't know."

"You can't be so concerned about failure. No one accomplishes everything that they desire, but there are things you feel compelled to do and you have to chase those aspirations."

"I will then."

"Seriously?"

"Yes, I'll think about it," I reluctantly replied.

21

ithin two weeks, Cora and I boarded a train to Columbia, 180 miles away. At her urging I made an appointment at the University of Missouri. We were discussing dreams the morning after that dance in the rain and I admitted to my love that my ambition to fly was strong but unlikely. Yet, being the wonderful breath of inspiration that she always is, Cora said 'you must at least try!' And so we rode the rails, together, and tossed to-and-fro ideas on arranging my admission.

"You have to speak of your passion for flying," she encouraged.

"Ok…but aren't they looking for more than just my interest? Like my background, my primary studies, my pocketbook?"

"Well…no…maybe…I don't know—it doesn't matter! Just work what you have and I'm telling you it's important, extremely important, to them that you care and are passionate, driven, focused."

"Right. And I would give it my all, had I the opportunity."

"Of course you would. Do line it up for yourself. Go get the opportunity!"

"Thanks," I grinned. "You're sure swift at cheerleading."

Little girl giggles.

"What's your greatest dream?" I wondered aloud.

"Hmm." She thought for a moment but I could tell she already plainly knew; the answer on the edge of her tongue, eagerly ready

204

to pass through her lips. "Honestly to be a wife. That's ultimately all I've wanted. Sure you can say that I'd enjoy writing in whatever free time I'd have. I'd say I'd expect very little as a wife and mother but what-can-you-do," she laughed. "Mostly I'd like to concentrate on composing and lyricism. But probably keep variety with short stories, perhaps a novel, and something for the stage."

"That's great."

"Hmm. Uh-huh."

"No, truly, Cora. Your focus is impressive but not rigid. It's perfect, you're perfect; you have that sweet balance of feminine submission and admirable ambition."

"Thank you so much!" she emphatically proclaimed with the utmost sincerity. "I've waited *so long* to hear a man say that."

I smiled.

Our comfort in one another's presence was unmistakably apparent. An elderly couple sitting adjacent to us in the dining car noticed it, with tender pleasure. The elder gentleman smiled through his eyes at me, denoting his approval in the bond between Cora and me; I respected it wholeheartedly—he was married nearly for life, you see.

That night we stayed in the common car and sat beside one another, staring through the window at the black sky and faint stars. Telling more stories we passed the time and burned through the early morning hours. Yet at one point I interrupted my own seemingly-never-ending story and turned to view Cora's expression. She, however, was fast asleep and immediately I silenced myself. Tipping my ivy cap over my eyes I nodded off, finally in real peace. How funny, sleeping in a quiet room, alone, deep in my soft bed and plush covers wasn't anywhere close to as comfortable as that rocky train, unpadded chair, lights overhead, and strangers barging by. Cora close to me enabled real rest like I hadn't realized I needed, until after the experience.

When we awoke Cora said, "We can make this happen."

"What's that, hon?"

"Piloting."

"Ah…you're still thinking about that huh?" Never previously had I been on another's mind, morning, noon, and night. *God, it felt electrifying.*

"Sure, you have to plan your goals, you can't just count on them working themselves out on their own."

"I see," I flirted. She blushed slightly and we paused for two minutes of awkward, invigorating sexual tension.

The trip was long and somewhat of a drag but once we arrived I comprehended what truly occurred. I hopped off the tracks and lugged our bags to a nearby bench. Cora wanted to powder her nose and pin-up her hair. In that few minutes apart I missed her terribly. It nearly surprised me. We had connected further, more intimately emotionally, and soothingly adjusted in one another's physical presence. My eyes even watered. *Damn it, stop.*

"Is everything alright?" Cora uttered to my back as I turned away to dab my eyes. "Jonathan?" she touched my back and the drops resumed.

"I'm fine," I insisted, facing her directly. *Be truthful, you can at this point.* "I—I got a little choked up being apart from you, even for that second, because we've been around each other a lot, you know? It's silly, I realize. I'm probably just tired," *yeah that's it,* "or anxious about going to the university." She wasn't buying it, rightfully so.

"We've grown. Together. Neither of us can help our feelings now. It's a good thing!"

Cora, right, as always.

We rode a taxi to the school and took an hour long hiatus to eat at an adjacent diner. I cleaned up my look and slammed down plenty of coffee to raise me to my best game. At last, I could delay it no more.

Cora's urging, "We need to go now, and catch the dean during the hours his secretary mentioned over the--"

"Ok," I snapped. Regaining my composure and flashing Cora an apologetic glance I said, "Let's go, love."

We traversed the damp one-lane street to the entrance of Jesse Hall. I just about choked in fear, my guts churning within, my soles glued to the pavement.

"What's the matter?"

"Not feelin' too tops, Cora."

She sighed in obvious frustration. "You can do this, I'm telling you." She wrapped her palms around my forearm as though we were attending a symphony and I was gentlemanly guiding my date inside. "We're here to try. What you have to do is sincerely put your faith and energy into your pursuits but not so much that you can't take heart if things fall short. We'll always pick ourselves up and move on."

I knew she was right, even if it fell short in soothing my anxiety.

We traipsed inside and skated coolly up the stairwell. Cora planned our journey prior to departing and it served me well now. At this point, adding time to locate a campus map or obtain directions from a faculty member or hurriedly-looking student would have pushed me into a full-blown nervous fit. At Cora's leading we stood before the entrance door to Dean Manfred's office summarily. His secretary caught sight of us through the side glass pane in the door, forcing me to not waver in the hall too long.

"Go in and do your best; I believe in you."

I nodded firmly and grabbed the brass handle. Confidently I turned it and entered into my fate, only peering back to see Cora alone, posing supportively. *Do this for her, for all she has done for you.*

"May I help you?"

"Yes. Ma'am. Um, I'm here to speak with Dean Manfred. I don't have an appointment per se, but he is expecting my arrival."

"Certainly." She jotted my name via pencil and yellow scratch paper and rushed away from her desk. "Excuse me, sir."

"Of course."

Three achingly-long minutes later she returned, addressing me with a masculine directness. "He'll see you now."

"Excellent. Thank you kindly." I bowed; I didn't know what else to do. It was my best, and most feeble, attempt at equivalent confidence.

I strolled behind the secretary, Betsy was presumably her name, I noted it on a postcard from San Francisco leaning against a rear bookshelf. She weaved to the left side of the chocolate-wood doorframe, and I was on my own to fight my scholastic battle.

"How do you do?" The elder gentleman spoke, addressing me forthrightly as he adjusted his glasses and patted down his immaculately greased and combed hair.

"Very well, sir," I replied, shaking his hand firmly although, frankly, his strength exceeded my own.

"Have a seat, young man." He motioned towards the dusty wooden chair in front of his desk and I expected him to mosey around and have a seat across from me. Yet, rather, Dean Manfred leaned atop his desk in front of me and began speaking. "I understand you've set up this appointment because you are interested in pursuing a career in flight?"

"Well, I'd like to, yes."

"Hmm. And what is your education status presently?"

How to answer…how to answer. "Nothing at this time. Nothing formal, I should say."

"I see. Well," he removed his glasses, breathed on them at close range, and wiped the fog away using the top corner of his orange and brown cardigan. He slowly held them up to the light and, presumably pleased with their cleanliness, repositioned them on his face. "It is uncommon to admit individuals who have not completed primary school and a score of undergraduate coursework…and shall I say not only completed but excelled--"

The Dean stopped himself mid-sentence. "I don't mean to discourage you."

"Oh, no, sir. It's certainly not an issue. You aren't being discouraging, simply honest…And, anyway, it's impossible to dishearten me."

"Is that so?"

"Yes, actually," I stated with a healthy level of confidence, nothing gratuitous.

"I like that, son. No one should ever underestimate the value of personal drive."

"I agree!"

He looked me over once more.

"Tell me, what can I do to ensure you are prepared should you encounter the opportunity and the funding to accept this challenge?"

"It's not what you can do, but what I can."

"Ah."

"I don't mean to insult you, Dean, and I hope you do not see it as such."

"Certainly. Would you wish to elaborate?"

I obliged. "Just that I am willing to do anything and everything to make this happen and, although I'm sure you hear a speech like this pretty frequently, I'm serious about the commitments I make, I've never shied away from hard work, and frustration to the point to quitting is absolutely not a part of who I am."

"That's good."

I was thirsting for more of a positive reaction than that but as usual I'll take what I can get.

"I won't disappoint you or myself if you'll simply crack the door of prospect for me here. That's all I am seeking. But if you cannot, I understand, and I thank you sincerely for your time."

"And then what shall you do? What will be your next avenue of pursuit?"

"To be honest, I don't have the details laid out yet, but I will, and I assure you I will charge head-first down that avenue you speak of." I stood up and composed myself; I extended my hand for a departing handshake but, surprisingly once more, his hand was not mutually extended.

"Sit down please…for just a few additional moments."

"Of course."

Dean Manfred stretched, wiped his brow, and sat again beside me.

"Young man what I will tell you in my many years of teaching and learning is that there are few things more important in academia—and in life—than self-motivation and self-education. If you can somehow capture the self-motivation you have towards this, and mix it with the preparatory skills you need for university studies, then I will take the chance on you, solely on your exhibited desire alone."

"Why thank you!" I bellowed in excitement. "What a way to knock my socks off. Thank you, sir, thank you so much!" I shook his hand with rapidity and muscle and he grinned despite the painful grip.

We parted with fair words and, upon wishing me well, the Dean sent me on my way. The second I emerged into the hallway Cora was all over me.

"What happened! What happened?!" She erupted while rocketing towards me, slapping my arm to denote the desire for an instant answer, despite her unwillingness to pause for my response. "Well?! What did he say? Was he impressed? At least…will they let you study?" Finally her surge ceased. "Ok, so tell me."

I beamed. "Everything went well, I mean, really well Cora. It was better than I thought--"

"Well you're a pessimist," she half-teased. "Continue."

"I don't know, there was something about me he must have appreciated." *Insert image of Cora jumping up and down, clapping her hands cyclically, chirping 'ooh yes' to all within an earshot.* "There's a few measures I can commit to so that I'll be ready, but I'm prepared to do that, you know?"

"Of course you are!"

"I'll make it happen; I—I'm ready!"

"Of course you will!"

"We will." I tightly gripped both her hands within my own.

"We will," she said, barely able to force the words through her shivering lips.

"I wouldn't be here without you Cora. And you know it."

"No I don't. You would! You would be here."

"Cora, listen to me…Are you listening?"

She nodded, her hands still encompassed within my own.

"This sounds campy, and I'm sorry for that part of it, but you have *completely turned my life around.* I had nothing…I've *had* nothing for as long as I can remember. And it's only because of your goodness that I'm doing more than surviving. To rebound from rail-riding, lonely nights, no prosperity, and, worst of all, the great depression *within*—hopelessness—is a tribute to the powers of a damn good woman."

We shrieked and I hoisted her in my arms, squeezing with no concern for the grip on her rib cage. I said 'I love you, I love you…' in conscious repetition, and we swayed to and fro in our corporal bond. Cora melded to my frame, and my mind at long last recognized that we were in a public setting.

"Um, should we get out of here?"

"Yeah," she giggled, her self-awareness resurfacing as well.

We paraded through the school grounds, equally confident and humble, further bonded by another life success. I was amazed, as accustomed, at all that we could do together that we would never accomplish apart.

As we returned home I watched Cora sleep and I thought of all these things and more. *Those words of gratitude that are inexpressible no matter the effort put forth to select them.* I don't imagine I'll remember much about the trip back other than that one particular thought. We arrived, oddly refreshed, and one would assume we would be parting ways for the time being. And then Cora, standing vis-à-vis with me at the boardinghouse, glanced off into the courtyard, bewildered.

"Whatcha see?" I asked.

"Look. A wedding."

I turned and, sure enough, there was a couple standing in the sloped, dewy field, hand-in-hand and eyes fixed upon one another. Cora gripped my arm and jerked it towards her.

"Let's watch!" she demanded.

Nary a word of compliance or hesitation, I followed her to what appeared to be a somewhat private event.

"I'm not sure we should," I whispered to her.

"Don't be silly…everyone from the house is out here."

We stood with the wayfarers, this collection of transients, all equally captivated by this elusive, binding, ceaseless concept known as *love.*

"How can it be that two people find one another, from such unlikely backgrounds and roadways?" Cora wondered aloud.

"I don't know," I thoughtlessly replied, staring back at my own little miracle.

"We're on these paths in life, thousands of different roads to take, ways to go, and yet two people can meet up and, *poof,* become passengers on the same journey."

"Yes."

"It's truly amazing!"

"That, it is."

We savored the observance although my face apparently evoked the perplexity I felt within. Cora, once and again, questioned the odd look I conveyed.

"Well, what do you mean? It's nothing."

"It's not nothing. What's wrong? Your face is fossilized!"

"I guess I'm merely deep in thought, Cora."

"Oh yeah?" she toyed, extending her arms around my waist, pulling me close enough to bore into her twinkling eyes. "And what, pray tell, could you be thinking about at this-here wedding?"

Let down your guard, man.

"Y-you…you and I…I mean."

"Oh?" she coquetted.

"This is worth celebration, you know? Two people lost within one another, nary a thought preoccupying them but their adoration for their beloved. Marriage is a commitment based upon someone's heart and I have never forgotten that. There's so much futility and injustice in the world, but this, *this*, sure wipes it away."

"I agree," Cora whispered, leaning up to kiss my cheek, which I obliged.

We then witnessed the remainder of the nuptials. After the long, sacred kiss we greeted the couple with applause and well wishes. And yet, as you might have guessed, my soon-to-be mortification nearly ruined the pleasant scene.

"Tamara! Congratulations!" I echoed to the bride. She vigorously shook my hand and then proceeded with her introduction to Cora. The scene was a flurry of handshakes, informal kisses, and jubilant cheers. Within five minutes I deducted that I had greeted nearly every visitor on that field.

"And who are you?" Cora spoke to me, her hand extended and the most enchanting smirk painted on her fair face.

"I am nobody," I replied.

Immediately the few standing round me turned in shock and aversion at my comment.

"Excuse me?" Cora blurted.

"Nothin'," I dismissed.

She hauled me aside; clearly, the night had been corrupted.

"Don't *ever* feel that way about yourself, do you hear me?!"

"Yes."

"Huh?!"

"Yes!"

"Ok." Cora feverishly yanked my arms and I was lip-locked to my beloved. She had saved me again.

We returned to the festivities and scooped up a couple slices of white wedding cake. Cora jigged onto the tire swing and began devouring the frosting, scraping off clumps with her dessert fork and licking the flipside with her exposed, salivating tongue. What can I say, it was precious.

"It's a kaleidoscopic world," eventually she divulged.

I chuckled. "Oh is it?"

"Yah!" The fork-licking perpetuated.

"Do you care to expatiate?" I laughed; gratified to use one of the words Cora had taught me.

She replied, "It's from the Dreiser book, Jennie Gerhardt. He writes about American color and energy. All the different people from various walks of life, it's they who comprise the American spectrum--"

"Right. Sure."

"--and, providentially *and* sadly, it's because of this fact exactly that appearances are worth something. Or so he says and I do, verily, agree."

Saying nothing, I'm certain the look on my face beamed "yes, I see."

It's funny how life works. The second we feel peace, an upsetting act may occur. At the moment of our deepest hopelessness, love enters our lives. In the minute of one's worst need, an hour absent of poverty may present itself. Or so this is what I have seen. And this distinct evening was no deviation.

As Cora and I finished our cake, moseyed hand in hand on the misty grass, soaked in the coral sunset and warm laughter of the guests, those known and unknown, bitter news crept from the main house. A Cherokee passerby, acknowledged only as Phoenix, drank himself to death in his room. He was a man I scarcely knew, just an uncomplicated nod "hello" here and there. It wasn't a secret by any means that he drank; one could categorically smell it on him. But why, why *that night*, did he set his spirit free from this earth? Was it the dolor of being alone at a wedding, I wondered. I'd never know, but I vowed to give him the respect that I could and bring joy out of his sorrow. To Cora, I clung, in Phoenix's honor.

22

$\mathcal{I}$t probably goes without saying, but the wedding was a revelation. Cora's eyes transfixed to the event and I knew, during the entire course of that evening, that she would wish to talk about it again and again that same night.

After we snuck upstairs, Cora wiped away her makeup using the simply Ivory soap in my washroom and changed into her long nightshirt. Her hair pinned up loosely to the back of her head, she finally addressed the thought at the forefront of her mind.

"You know," she began. "You wouldn't really consider that to be a very romantic wedding, but it was, wasn't it."

"Yes," I reassured, as harmoniously as I possibly could.

"Why did you believe it to be so?"

"So romantic?"

"Yeah!!" Obviously Cora was anxious to get to the meat of this discussion.

"Because they truly wanted to marry one another."

"Right! All I kept noticing was how the surroundings were wet and dirty and undecorated and there were people shuffling around, smoking, whispering, and there weren't any high-class musicians or gourmet foods…or even a champagne toast! But, still, they looked so, *so* happy. It was remarkable; it was what I'd wish for anyone, for myself. Indeed, I'll never forget it."

"Mmm," I concurred.

A moment of silence and then, "well what shall we do tonight?" from Cora, in her merriest voice.

"I don't know. It wasn't enough excitement for you to witness nuptials and then sneak into my room for the evening?"

Then, those girlish giggles, which I adore.

"There is, believe it or not, one more thing which I absolutely, unequivocally, must have for tonight!"

"Really now. And what could this possibly be?"

"Come here!"

She flopped back onto my bed and, emulating a sweet seductress to the best of her abilities, Cora announced "I expect you to hold me this night, Jonathan."

"I can oblige you for that, missy."

"Ha ha…but only cuddling."

"Of course."

We lay, unwontedly deprived of one another. There was always present the need Cora and I shared for each other's consolation. I spooned her languid frame, my fingers skating along her slender bones, and repeatedly I inhaled the smell of her redolent, distaff hair.

"I could lie like this forever," she said.

"So why don't you?"

Mirthfulness.

"No, I'm serious. What's stopping you Cora?"

"What do you mean!"

"Whaddya mean 'what do I mean'?"

"You're confusing me."

"No. You're confusing yourself." We cachinnated. "You're complicating things."

"Oh is that so?"

"Yes. Women tend to do that."

"It's all so easy to you, then?"

"Of course. You want me. I want you. What else is there to consider?"

I ciphered she wanted to respond. Her lips quivered momentarily but no words broke forth. She sought to dismiss my point, but she knew that she could not.

"I suppose you are right," she whispered.

"What's that? I can't hear you," I proclaimed haughtily, my hand cupping my ear to amplify her acknowledgement.

"You're ridiculous!"

"Am I?" I knew I was being silly. But our banter was most rapturous this go-around.

I grabbed her hand and held it to my heart. She appeared shocked and too slow to react. A moment passed and I raised her fingers to my lips and kissed the tips. There, they remained and my muggy, mild breath steamed her skin.

We said very little over the next hour or so. Simply put, we pawed, smiled, dallied, and relaxed. I made us both a cup of breakfast tea, it was all I had, and then I hoisted two windows so we could hear the jazz tunes emanating from the front porch.

"Would you care to dance?"

"I would."

And we did.

23

The next six months are practically indescribable. Sure, I could attempt it. Yes, I might draw you in further. And, granted, you'd know even more about this lovely woman and myself, enraptured in one another. But, why explain it...explanations are needless.

We talked. We acceded. We disagreed. We compromised.

We laughed. We teased. We canoodled. We parted.

We reunited. We hoped. We planned. We were.

Then, one day, "what are you afraid of?" she asked me for an off-the-cuff list.

"Hmm...I suppose..." I began, "I am afraid of one thing and one thing alone: that you are too good to be true."

She soaked it in and thought upon it. I could decode, however, that she wasn't vexed because her side-smirks always give away her internal at-ease. All, still well.

"And what, for you? I bet you have an extensive list," I half-kidded.

"My only fear is abandonment. Period."

"I know. No worries, love."

"None."

This is all too easy.

It's staggering how good things can be in reality. One doesn't require fantasy to live gratified and vindicated. Just the opposite, indeed. Reality presents itself in the most abating of terms, as just the simplest hand-hold, dutiful word, uproarious quip, or reciprocated hope can comfort any breathing flesh *any night* of the week.

Then, one afternoon, Cora said, "Why do you believe we met? Fate?"

I had changed, markedly so. One could allude because I replied, "Fate."

Never previously would I indulge said thought for another.

"Count all the ways you love me," she cooed.

"That would be mighty difficult."

"Difficult is good. Do it regardless."

"Your mind, one; your spirit, two; your beauty, three; your kindness, forth…this could take all day long, I tell you."

"You don't have to then," she sweetly resigned.

"Oh, but I do."

"Quit joshing me!" Laughter.

"I'm not, love. It's no joke to say that I need to tell you why you are so perfect for me."

"I think we both know."

"Agreed, again."

I then mentioned to Cora the story of one of my heroes, John Stevens.

"Now you're going to think I'm nothing like him, but humor me and follow along anyway."

"Of course," she giggled.

"So here is this guy, Colonel Stevens, officer of the Revolution, born before the Declaration, before the U.S. as we know it. Yeah, he was born into money, studied at Columbia, became a lawyer, an engineer. Huge estate the size of a Jersey city. But! He, remarkably so…right?, was just purely and wholeheartedly devoted to the study and policy of cross-country travel. The potential lying within the rails was immeasurable to him and so Stevens said, 'hey, let's not think old with canals, let's go for the new and think of steamships and power rails.' I could give you all the details about the screw propellers and boilers and circular tracks, but you wouldn't be interested, no doubt, no offense! Anyway...I didn't point out the neatest part of it all."

"What's that?"

"Well, the man was 75 before he finally crafted the first steam loco in the States."

"Is that so?"

"Uh huh."

"Whew." *She was impressed, as was I.*

"My points are these. One, I admire the man for his ingenuity and determination--"

"Right!"

"and, two, like Coolidge says, 'nothing in this world can take the place of persistence'."

"Amen to that, my love."

I sighed. And was silent, both in words and expression.

She paused, searching my face. I could tell she was trying to discern why my mood altered so spontaneously.

"Did something happen, er, are you alright?"

"Yes." I waited. "I just want you to understand why I mentioned this story."

"Oh, yes, I know that everything you say to me has meaning behind it."

"I know," I encircled her hand. "All I want to prove to you is that I may not be the man that I need to be for you right now, but one day, I will. Don't give up on me, Cora. It's all I ask of you and, granted, it's a lot to ask of anyone. But one day, goddamn it, if I'm 75 years old, I'll assume my potential."

She lit up.

"Sorry for the cursing."

"No problem." She grinned again. "I could not believe in you any more than I do, Colonel."

24

She surprised me again.

"This is for you," Cora blurted as she plopped a medium-sized box, wrapped in plain brown paper with a bright blue ribbon and bow enveloping it, into my clumsy hands. I nearly dropped it.

"Woah," I gagged.

"Don't drop it, it'll break."

"Really?" I was alarmed and embarrassed.

"No," she fooled.

I let out a short laugh. "May I open it?" I questioned as I gestured to the package.

"Certainly." She refrained from any additional sarcasm, though I realized she was eager to continue the antics.

The bow slipped apart with one small tug and, like silk, it unraveled off the package onto the floor. Neglecting it, I ripped off the thick basic paper like a five year old on Christmas confident of the present that lay underneath.

There, in my hands, an old man's hat box.

"Take off the lid," my girl whispered.

It was a pilot's hat. Thunderstruck, yet only for a moment.

"Oh yes!" I gibbered and howled. Blathering on, I pas-de-bourréed, making a scene, and stuffed the topper on my crown. Snuggly I settled the brim.

"Do I look dapper?" I posed haughtily like a catalog model.

"Yes, definitely spiffy--"

"It's swell, thanks, love!"

"You are quite welcome. I'm glad you like it, it's plumb smart on you!"

Giggles.

"Well I *look* the part!"

"I want you to do more than play a part, J. It's your pursuit, and a good one at that."

"Aces," I coolly schmoozed.

For day after blessed day, I sported the hat proudly on our outings. Heck, I wore it around town everywhere, and at home as well. I donned it while shaving, as I made toast, even for a morning bathroom run, thank-you-very-much.

That Saturday morning, we walked.

"Still enjoying the look?" I flirted with Cora, posing with a fox-grin and my hand propped markedly under my hat.

"Yes, love it!"

We kicked around town, ending up at the boys' ball field sharply at noon. A pickup game was in its early stages. The boys raced through the dirt, leaving tiny earth clouds in their shadows. They pummeled the hard ball with their worn sticks, slivering their hands and jolting the park's more peaceful inhabitants.

"Go, Jerry, run!"

"Get that ball, Andy. Get it!"

"I've got it guys...look!"

Their cries reported all that was special with respect to the sounds of summer: youngsters laughing, an old man passing-by whistling, two ladies cooing at well-fed pigeons, the warm wind gently swaying blossomed trees.

I approached the neighborhood team.

"You boys see that tree trunk over there?" I pointed at a fairly substantial, albeit dead, stump close to three hundred or so feet away.

"Yeah, sure," a few of them chimed together.

"Watch me, I'm gonna knock this ball right past there. Who's throwin'?"

"Me!" one fervent boy jumped.

I positioned myself at home plate, squinting to avoid the yellow midday glare, and drew the bat back, floating it over my right shoulder. The boy let the pitch loose.

Crack!

It soared through the humid air and clopped onto the rear of the tree trunk. Quickly it rolled off the wood, resting on the grassy patch, hiding it from our view.

"Where is it?" one boy teased.

"Oh, you saw it!" I shot back.

"Nice comeback," Cora retorted.

I gave her a sly squint.

"Yeah, I did it, youngsters!" I smarted. "I'm quite the sportsman, I must admit myself, I--"

A mob of the spry athletes jetted to Jonathan's back. Two jumped aboard and he shrieked in both shock and soreness.

"Hey now, fellas, there's no need to attack me here!"

He wrestled with a few of them, amidst a sea of energetic laughter and dirt-stained tees and slacks. It was heart-gratifying. *Should I jump in too?* There was something I needed to say in that moment; I struggled to withhold.

So, like a burst of hurricane wind, I burrowed my way through the crowd, tugging at the back of Jonathan's disheveled shirt.

"Hey!"

Despite all the contiguous noise, he turned to me immediately and quite bewildered at my impoliteness, uttered "huh" and nothing more.

I thought, quickly, of what I longed to say.

"I want all of this!" I demanded.

"You can have it! You will!" he shouted. And, then, in a melodious, comforting tone…"Please just hang in there with me."

I nodded, in full agreement.

25

J had the best-laid of intentions.

"We're going to the fair!" I proclaimed, expecting a jubilant reply of gratitude from Cora.

"The fair?" she questioned as though she had never heard of such a thing.

"Y-yes," I stumbled, perplexed.

"Oh. The town fair. Oh. Ok."

"Is there a problem? Were you tortured as a child by face-painting clowns or popcorn salesgirls?" I fooled.

She chuckled, charmed.

"No, no," resoundingly, she replied. "Going to the fair will suit me just fine."

"Well then what was with your initial reaction, silly?"

"Oh, it *is* silly, nevermind."

"Tell me," I flirted, while tickling her facetiously.

"I'm not much of a fan of carnival rides, J."

"Oh! So you're scared!" I toyed with her insecurity, probably a little too much. Luckily for me, she let it pass.

"Yes, I suppose," she humbly stated.

"Let's give it a go," I cheered, "and if you're not havin' a swell time, we'll jolt. How's that sound?"

"Great," she bargained.

So on that breezy Friday evening we strolled composedly to the town square. The entire park, usually a sparse, cubic, plain grass patch, was covered foot to foot with twinkling lights, machinery and cords, prizes and corresponding games, trash bins, occupied benches, and, most of all, the scurrying feet of high school pranksters, excited youth, tight-knit families, and couples in love. We belonged in that last group, *youshouldknow.*

"This looks like a lot of fun," I encouraged.

"It's a whole lotta excitement, certainly."

Cora clenched my arm, half in attempt to avoid physical separation, the other to secure her footing. But then she danced around thick cables and tent posts, hopping and contouring as needed, slithering through the marching crowd all the while.

"Hey, don't forget about me." I was a little ill at ease of letting loose my beauty in this brood.

"Sorry!" she cooed, melting my ego.

"It's ok. I don't want us to get split up…that wouldn't be fun." Straight away I was on the verge of tears. *What's wrong with me?! Damn, this girl has a hold.*

We stopped, staring intensely at one another.

"Do you want to go on a ride?" I could see Cora intuited that she needed to break the silence with a proposition.

"Maybe later." It was time to kiss her, not plan the evening.

Her lips tasted fresh and sinuous, once more it seemed as though we had never previously embraced.

"Come with me on a ride," I lit up.

"Err--"

"Please, Cora. You'll--"

"Have fun, I know!" Her sarcasm led me to believe she was growing tired of my pressings. But her sensibility reemerged. "I'm going to pass, J."

"Really?!"

She paused momentarily, glancing at the fair's tallest, fastest demon...a twirling, racing ride of four-person pods that could very well leave the strongest man puny afterward. As it rocked, Cora's eyes widened, her ears peaked by the frantic shouts of the tense boarders.

"Ok, Jonathan, I'm not afraid anymore." She pierced through my eyes, concreting her seriousness. *God, I love this woman.*

Silence on my behalf, and then we smiled in unison.

"So, let's go then," I beamed, scooping her little hand and leading her to our challenge.

Shriiiiieeeekkkks!!

"That...was...exhilarating!" she cheered upon annihilation of her fear.

I barely had my footing.

"Sugared apples next!" she tweeted.

"Um...ok." My stomach was in my throat. A candy-covered confection? Sure, why not.

Cora danced her way in line, hoisting onto her toes to catch a better glimpse of the treats for sale. She turned around and smiled eagerly at me. I was missing her and we were only half a dozen yards apart.

"Do you want me to wait in line with you?"

"No!...But you can wait in line *for* me, ha ha!"

"Ahh, ok. Why is that my love?"

"Just to be funny!"

I joked.

"I'm kidding! I'm off to freshen up. Be back in a jiff." Then she recited her order to me, as though I was unaware. "One sugared apple for your girl!"

Just as swiftly, she darted to the ladies' room.

I purchased our apples; *sure I got one too*, and then fumbled my way through the crowd to meet up with Cora. I understand how girls are but, jeez, she was sure takin' her time in the bathroom!

"Jonathan?" Yet, that wasn't Cora's voice emerging behind the dirty, ivory door.

"Oh. Stephanie. Hi." *Please, leave. Please, leave. Please.*

"How have you been?"

I nodded, signifying "well."

"Who are you here with? Or is one of those apples for me?" She reached out her hand; I darted the apples behind my forearm and jerked myself a foot back.

She roared with giggles. "Aww, that's delightful. But I was only foolin'!"

"Oh. It's for Cora. My girlfriend. Cora."

"Yes. I met her in the ladies' room."

"How? How did you know it was her? And you were you? I mean, how did she know you are you? You know what I mean!" *Damn, spill it already, woman!*

"Well, I saw you speaking with her earlier. So I asked. She's so sweet! I was listening and then I figured you'd be out here, the gentleman that you are, so I popped out and--"

"Here's your apple, baby." Cora was at long last back beside me. I, noticeably, was on the verge of dour heart palpitations due to my Stephanie-nerves. I gave Cora a look that said *I can't believe our beautiful night was ruined by an unwanted visitor.*

"Thanks, sugar! Hee hee." She bopped me on the nose with her apple and then dug in for a hearty bite. "Mmm.." she delighted. She grinned all the while chopping away and licking her lips. "Juicy, sweet, and oh-so good!...Try yours!"

She was adamant, so I sunk my teeth into the goody. It was delicious, just a little sour for my already-turned stomach.

"'Ts good," I grumbled.

Cora teeheed once more and I percolated if Stephanie was jealous or truly contented for me to be with this peerless woman. There wasn't much time to wonder, however, because as quickly as she came to disturb us, Stephanie disappeared. Time to read Cora's mood. *Nothing.*

"So, she was nice."

"Yeah," I answered, merely for conversational purposes. Don't know whether I actually agreed.

I thought for a moment.

"She's alright. A little artificial for my taste."

"That's ok," Cora remarked, still giggling, of course. "It was fine to see her. You're mine and knowing of her, it doesn't hurt anymore."

26

Then came the long-awaited night.

Have you ever had a moment of realization in which you surmised that a thousand little steps along various roads now led you to the place you had been long searching?

Tonight, for me, was that night.

As we approached Compari's for dinner I wondered if Cora shared in said awakening.

"Be seated," the mâitre d' oozed to Cora, pulling her chair from behind her, positioning it like an artist gently easing a small sculpture onto its permanent platform.

Had I been privy to such beauty before?

"You look stunning."

"You always say that!" she dismissed.

"Yes, and I always mean it...But tonight--"

She waited.

"Tonight--"

Again I paused.

"--I say it as though I've never spoken the word before. Stunning."

She sighed, half-uncomfortably. But I knew she was flattered.

"What do you anticipate ordering?" Cora hurriedly changed the subject.

"I don't know, we shall see, my dear!"

Everything on the menu was in Italian.

"Was this to be expected?" I goofed.

"It is an Italian restaurant, after all, Jonathan."

"Your logic is adorable. And so is the rest of you. And so is pol-pe-t-tone di car-n-e cru-da."

"Do you even have a clue what that is?" my girl giggled.

"No. What is it?"

"Oh, I don't know!" she sung.

"Great, we'll both have it!"

After relishing in our fried meatballs and pasta Romano, Cora insisted on cappuccino and tiramisu.

"I can't pronounce this dessert either, but it's delicious!" I scooped a heavy bite of the luscious cream and sweet, soggy cookies, and furled it into my mouth. Cora didn't look the least bit displeased but I hurriedly second-guessed my decision to eat like a starved beast in front of her.

"And what shall we do next, monsieur?" Cora quipped. "Oh wait. Monsieur is French. What's mister in Italian?"

I sat in reflection. *Like I'm gonna come up with this!*

"Signore, young lady!" A senior waiter spouted from across the way.

We blushed.

"Well, señorita," Cora looked at me funny. *Yes, that was Spanish, but whatever.* "I thought we could take a little walk back to my place."

"Oh...Is there a present awaiting me?"

Think of something! No, be honest.

"No. There isn't. But I'd like more time with you with tonight."

She smiled unabashedly. "Sounds wonderful."

I settled our bill, repeatedly thanked our server for the excellent meal, and guided Cora to the front door. We left, satisfied with our dinner and one another, equally.

Slowly we coasted down the empty streets to my home. I finally self-affirmed that I had met my match; Cora, my lifelong co-passenger.

When we crossed the rusted, dinged-up train tracks, Cora stopped.

"Oh-ha!" I exploded in hilarity. "You should never stop on train tracks," I outburst in my best know-it-all voice.

She failed to reply.

"You ok?" Now I was concerned.

"Oh, sure," she whispered, still staring at the metal below. She dusted the sand from one portion of a track, using only the tip of her right toes.

Something wasn't right.

"Can you tell me why we're halted?" I thought the night was going well.

"No reason," she smiled. "I didn't mean to worry you. I—I'm still in a good mood, J."

"Well, whatcha thinkin' about?"

"Us."

"Really?"

"Yeah. I saw the train tracks and it just hit me!"

"What did?"

"The memories that we have together. A lot of them are connected to the trains, you know?"

"Yes."

"The stories you've shared with me, the places we've gone… and now we're this old couple, aged like these railway runners and ties."

"That's a good thing, Cora!"

"I agree. It just choked me up a tad, that's all."

"You know, a lot of people don't realize this but the railways need to be maintained."

"Oh?"

"Yes. So often people think trains can glide across anything, no matter how broken down the structure appears to be. But, there's a science involved." She was listening intently, I could tell. "You need a good foundation."

"And we have that," Cora confidently chimed in.

"We sure do, baby doll."

We returned, hand in hand, to my place. So comfortable with one another, as you can only be when you have met your match.

For an hour or so, *who keeps track of time*, I sat beside Cora, brushing her hair from her forehead, listening to additional stories, smiling allthewhile at her humor and candor.

We kissed on a number of occasions, and it was exhilarating.

Then, I decided to ask.

"Would you like to lay in bed with me? We could just relax or I could hold you. I want to."

"I really do, too."

We settled on top of the covers and continued to embrace. It was even more romantic than my ridiculous head had previously predicted. *More romantic than I'm telling you here, you see.*

She arose. Then, I stood as well.

Now, I was unaware of what to expect. Frozen, I fervently anticipated her next move.

27

When her hands went under the bottom hem of her skirt, I knew this was it. Something was coming off. This was the instant I had waited my life for and I knew once that skirt was raised, things would never be the same between Cora and me. As the peach linen lifted the way the sunrise catches you in awe on any given morning, fractions of her soft, milky legs were exposed. I had seen much of those legs previously, but never with this sort of anticipation. Then, in a flash, she dropped her skirt and the fabric came crashing down as though the weight of it was too much for her to hoist. *Should I offer my help?* I thought like an idiot.

"This will be easier," she whispered. Her dainty fingers unbuttoned the back of the skirt and she flung it onto the worn oak floor as though it was nothing. Her confidence in divulging herself was what I expected out of a wife who had stood uncovered before her husband countless times before.

With just her top on and cardigan buttoned overlaid, she slithered towards the bed. She paused on the edge, and finally made eye contact with me. Her hair and makeup were still flawless and her skin looked as though it had never been touched. Thinking of that energized me the most. She fiddled with her jewelry, as though in that moment she needed to decide whether to take it off forever or leave it on permanently. Then, in an instant she paused and I realized she had concluded the jewelry was insignificant. Cora rested comfortably and her green eyes escalated toward the copper-covered ceiling.

She peeled her lace panties back and I closely saw *something* which I had never seen before. I was speechless. It was good that no one had ever attempted to describe to me previously what *it* intimately looked like, because it was truly indescribable.

Cora resituated herself on top of the duvet and exhaled. I could see her flat tummy move as the air exited her frame. I, however, couldn't move.

I desperately wanted to go to her and at least be close to her body, even if I couldn't garner the will to touch it. But I couldn't move.

She laid there on her back, looking calm and a little cold. But most of all, she looked ready. Still, I was.

It seemed like hours had passed but it was probably only minutes later when one of us finally budged. She did not turn her head, nor shift her eyes onto me. It was as though her gaze had business with the copper tiles and they simply could not part ways. She merely moved in the slightest. Her knees inched apart and she fully exposed herself to me. *Holy fuck, I cannot breathe.* My eyes were affixed to the beauty between her legs.

Silence.

Silence.

Silence.

"Don't you want to come over here?" Her voice was dirtily seductive, another first.

Respond. Respond!

She giggled like a little girl.

"You don't have to say anything," she said. "Just walk over and sit beside me."

I did. I walked over and paused bedside. She patted the feathery duvet, indicating the place for my seating. I gasped and sat.

"This is yours now. I'm giving myself to you, Jonathan."

By *this* I assumed she meant her body, but I was clearly too drained of my intelligence to think properly.

"As your property, it is up to you to do with me as you wish." *Damn, she was good at seduction.*

"And what do you wish for?" I heard her ask but how could I reply? Finally, my mind joined my body in the room.

"You've already given me what I wished for, Cora."

"Really?"

"Yes." Tears began flooding my eyes and I felt humiliated. It was the emotional culmination of all of our experiences together but, still, I did not want her to see me like this. I had to tell her to reassure her of my manhood. "I am not weak, don't read into this."

"Jonathan!" she snipped. "It is beautiful to be weak with your woman. I would never use anything against you."

"I hope not." *And, God, I meant it.*

"I wouldn't." Her tone was daringly serious, which soothed me. "I know you've been hurt before in ways I cannot reference. But I have had many difficulties in my life. And all I can say is that everything I went through was worthwhile to bring me to this one moment. This is the opportunity for me to have what I've truly always wanted--"

"Which is what?" I asked as though we had never embarked on this discussion previously.

"To be with the man I love and to feel his love in return. To give of my faithfulness and loyalty as I was always meant to give it."

"You are one of few women who are willing to wholeheartedly give it."

"I know. And you deserve it, Jonathan. For what you have never had, I will award you."

With those words she pulled me towards her. I hovered above her half naked body and allowed my lips to bond with hers. I tasted her breath and pushed more vigorously onto her mouth. I was desperate to show her she was loved.

As we kissed, my fingers slid behind her head and I caressed her silky hair. We kept kissing. Her arms wrapped around my waist as far as they could go and her miniscule nails gripped my lower back. I didn't know how far to take it until I opened my eyes mid-kiss and saw her staring back at me. This was it.

I leaned back to my knees and carefully crawled off the bed. I remained elevated beside the bed, my feet firmly planted as I sheathed my clothes mid-paced. Her smile was all the permission I needed.

At the last moment I stood before her in merely my under shorts. And I said, "Cora, I have something to give you." She was midway through unbuttoning her cardigan and paused. I instructed her to wait one moment and I scurried to my bag. She looked more excited than the first day I was introduced to her and, then, I thought that scene could never be duplicated. She removed her sweater and crept beneath the sheet and duvet. With lucid alacrity, she awaited my gift.

"Jonathan! What is it!" She tittered and clapped and her eyes glistened like marquise emeralds.

I darted back to my Cora with one hand behind my back. "Ready?" I said, only adding to the suspense.

"I know what it is!" she screamed.

"Oh no you don't!"

"Yes I do!!!"

"Um, ok, what?" My sarcasm was nearly as prevalent as hers.

"It's a train token! You always told me you would give me a train pass if you were in love with me." She sounded convinced. "I'm right! Aren't I! I'm right!" She began dancing arrogantly and the little boxer in Cora re-emerged.

"Nope." I was more poised than Cora for once. I reached out my hand and unveiled the mystery. It was my mother's wedding ring. By the look in her eyes and the silence from her lips I could tell she pieced together the significance on her own.

"Jonathan."

"Are you ready for this?" I asked her, reversing our roles from only an hour prior.

"Yes." She spoke definitively and I knew she was ready.

I lowered to my knees and clutched her trembling hand. The nerves hit me, but in a good way.

"Jonathan, you only have to be on one knee."

"No. For you, I'll be on both knees. You deserve it."

I smiled at her and said little. Only what was truly necessary.

"Cora, if you say yes we are husband and wife now. Forever. I will marry you in a church, with the ceremony you want, but that is simply a repeat of the commitment we are exchanging now. You've offered me your body and I wouldn't be the man for you unless I married you first. It's what we both want. So, Cora, will you marry me?"

The ring slid onto her petite finger and at once she clutched it to ensure it would stay on. She gawked at it, her eyes dancing over every jewel.

"Yes!"

And that was all I needed to hear.

We spent the rest of that night making love for the first time. I could tell you about every night thereafter and what happened as the years passed. But, I think, you already know.

About the Author

*C*assandra Swiderski is currently employed as an academic librarian in Warren, Michigan. She holds Master's and Doctorate degrees in library science and systematic theology, respectively, and has been the recipient of several scholarly and private writing awards for journalism, songwriting, playwriting, and poetry. *Passengers* is her first published novel.